Divine Wind

Lee Clinton

A Black Horse Western

ROBERT HALE

© Lee Clinton 2020
First published in Great Britain in 2020

ISBN 978-0-7198-3137-9

The Crowood Press
The Stable Block
Crowood Lane
Ramsbury
Marlborough
Wiltshire SN8 2HR

www.bhwesterns.com

Robert Hale is an imprint
of The Crowood Press

Typeset by
Simon and Sons ITES Services Pvt Ltd
Printed and bound in Great Britain by
4Bind Ltd, Stevenage, SG1 2XT

ONE

A LITTLE HELP

The Skidoo Pass – 1885

He felt the massive steel-rimmed wheel slip sideways towards the sheer edge of the narrow mountain pass, and like a scorpion upon his neck, ready to strike, it made Brodie's skin crawl with fear. It was the rear wheel of the first box wagon. The one taller than a man. It had suddenly skewed to the left by ten feet to gouge a deep trench into the weathered track. Instinctively, his fists tightened as he pulled back on the reins to slow the team of twenty mules. He didn't want them to stop. Not now, not up here, it was too dangerous. He needed them to keep their footing and give the steerage so necessary to get this juggernaut of two huge freight wagons and an iron-clad water tank down the steep incline to the valley floor five hundred feet below.

5

Brodie braced and sucked in a breath that burnt deep within his chest. It was as if the air had come from an open furnace. Why would any man want to work in this godforsaken place? Why would someone like Robert Brodie choose to make Death Valley his home? Some say fate – others, stupidity. Why does any man persist with disappointment?

He'd been a miner for longer than he cared to remember and only ever made enough to pay his way. When he finally stopped chasing gold at the end of a pick to become a muleskinner, those prospecting years seemed like nothing more than a bitter waste of time. A life sentence served for a crime he didn't commit. Where had the best part of twenty years gone?

Why had he stayed so long?

The Timbisha Shoshone Indians had been here longer, a thousand years or more. Their lives were just as hard, so what did Bob Brodie, the newcomer, the intruder, have to complain about? Was it because his stay had been unplanned? Much in life was for so many men after the war.

An overnight stop at Stovepipe Wells in '65 to water his mules – that's where it had started, on a return journey to California. It was there that he'd chanced upon a fellow traveller, a miner, who told of the silver and gold that lay in the desolate, but beautifully coloured mountains surrounding the valley. 'A fortune enough for every man,' he was told.

He shouldn't have listened.

He should have pulled politely on the brim of his hat and continued on his way the next morning as planned. What did he know about mining anyway? He was a lumberman by trade and a soldier out of what now seemed like a foolish sense of loyalty to Texas. It was his mother's state, her birthplace, not his. He should have moved on and returned to San Francisco, to his father's city, to find work back amongst the redwoods.

But he didn't.

Instead he went looking for that fortune that was there for every man, except him, and just about every other hole digger who burrowed deep into the side of those pastel pale mountains. The few traces of that glorious golden metal he was able to prize from the rocks were only ever enough to hint at what his pick may strike tomorrow. It was the enticement of the devil, urging him on, to keep digging for that elusive seam. Much like the tease of a beautiful woman from behind a veil, one who gave the eye to a thousand suitors with each believing her charms were meant just for them. Fools. They were all fools and Brodie knew he was one of the biggest.

Then came borax.

He'd seen the mineral deposits out on the pans and in the lower hills, dismissing those dirty white crystals as worthless. What possible purpose could they serve? Yet the Winters seemed to know when they staked their claim in '81.

Rose Winter was the smart one. Brodie could see it in her eyes, and she alerted him to the prospects. On nothing more than a whim, and a wink from Rose, he did the same and laid a claim. After all, what did he have to lose?

His deposits, like those of the Winters, proved to be pure grade and easy to mine. However, they were of little value until refined and to do that both know-how and capital were required. He had neither. When the Winters sold their holdings to the Harmony Borax Mining Company, who were building a refinery at Furnace Creek, he did the same.

To his surprise he received a better than expected return. Not a fortune but it was more than he'd accumulated over the past decade and a half. The irony that it had come from the unexpected sale of real estate was not lost on Brodie. Work hard and you fail, get lucky and you collect. Such is life – it will drive you into the ground then smile on you when least expected.

Was it a game being played from on high?

Regardless, it was his second chance. The means to leave the valley nearly eighteen years after stopping to water his mules at Stovepipe Wells. He counted up his wealth, rolled the notes tight and put them in a woollen sock along with his pebble-sized nuggets. He then packed up his belongings ready to leave for Frisco, set to reunite with his four sisters – when he stopped dead. Somehow, he had remembered to ask himself that simple question: then what?

He was going on 40, too old to start over on the end of an axe felling giant Northern Californian redwoods, and while his sisters would be happy to see him, they had their own families, their own lives. Maybe if his mother had still been alive it might have made a difference. Minnie had been gone some five years by then, leaving him with that sense of guilt that comes through careless neglect. He sat on the end of his bunk and mulled over the truth before quietly unpacking his possessions and preparing to go back into the mountains, back to prospecting for that once in a lifetime lucky strike.

Becoming a muleskinner had never crossed Brodie's mind, even though he'd worked mules for most of his life. Once he had worked a team of fifteen over near Badwater on a mine with a shaft close to half a mile long. He liked mules. Always did. They were smart, hardworking and trustworthy, and he liked how they got on with the job without complaint. Could they be cantankerous from time to time? Not enough for Brodie to notice, yet they had good reason if they wanted. Hauling an ore cart up and down a narrow mineshaft was hard, unrelenting work. What if it was full of gold; it weighed the same as rocks and dirt and they would never share in any reward.

When Harmony approached him to drive one of their mule teams pulling the massive borax wagons from the works at Furnace Creek to the railhead at Mojave, they were offering top wages. Few were interested in taking on the gruelling ten-day, 165-mile,

9

one-way trip through the heat and barren landscape. Of those who gave it a go, only a handful lasted. Though, if you could stick at it for a season or two, a small fortune could be made. This was now Brodie's third season and he had put away nearly every cent.

After all, what was there to spend it on?

Death Valley didn't even have its own saloon, let alone dancing girls. Out here, you worked and you slept, then worked some more. There was not much else, except for pork and beans most days and 48-card pinochle on Saturday night if you were crazy enough to risk your hand. If a drinking man, you could get a bottle of rotgut from the Furnace Creek general store that smelt of skunk piss and tasted like acid vinegar, and at a price that was sheer robbery. But at close to 100-proof it could temper the regrets of lost youth and the waste from a lost war. It also stopped those dreams, the ones that haunt the mind when in the deepest of sleeps.

Brodie's fists remained tight on the reins as the front wheel of the second wagon dropped into the rut carved into the mountain track by the first wagon. The spinning steel rim gouged out a deeper furrow towards the edge, churning and cutting as the tall sides of the huge box cart rocked, twisted and groaned in protest. Both wagons may have been empty, yet their huge, sturdy construction still made them more than a solid weight to haul for the twenty mules.

'Easy,' called Brodie, but who was he talking to? The wagon? The mules? There was nobody else. He was on his own. Just one man, a lone muleskinner clinging atop a wild serpent with a will of its own as the wagons shoved the team down the steep incline.

The mules, in pairs, were now beginning to slip upon the loose shale beneath their hoofs. Fear was present in the air and it showed in their upright ears and the whites of their eyes. This whole rig was close to sliding off the side of the mountain in a spectacular, tumbling, hurdy-gurdy of wagons and mules, with Brodie somewhere in the middle.

The third and final wagon, yoked and chained to the second, was the water tank for the mules. Built to hold 1,200 gallons, it now held half that, but it weighed a ton. Its first wheel dropped into the deep rut made by the other two wagons and the water within the long steel cylinder rushed like an ocean wave to the front of the tank. Some of the precious water shot up into the air from the top vent, which had become unlatched from the severe jolt.

The mules felt the strain as they dragged the wheel back out of the trench – but for only a moment. The rear wheel now dropped into the furrow, forcing the water to wash back. This immediate shift of weight was like a hammer blow upon an anvil as the immense force collapsed the whole side of the track beneath the water wagon. Earth, rocks and shale suddenly disappeared into space, to smash against the side of the mountain and explode into a cascading shower of stone fragments and dust.

Brodie heard the roar of the mountain and while he couldn't see the frightening spectacle, he and the mules could feel it. The outer rear wheel of the water wagon now hung in space and continued to turn for a second or two before it started to drop. Brodie slapped the reins and the mules responded, pulling hard. The accelerated pace of the team made the wagons shake violently and sway like a giant pendulum, about to swing the entire train off the pass and into mid-air. Was this serpent about to slither over the side of the mountain?

Brodie thought so and while not a man of prayer, at that very moment, without thought, he called to the heavens, 'God, I could do with a little help here.'

He didn't get an answer.

No voice came from on high through parting clouds, but something did happen that day that seemed most mysterious. The inside rear wheel of the water tank remained on good ground long enough for the outside wheel to defy gravity and find purchase back on the narrow mountain track. Immediately behind the wagons a giant chasm now appeared as the road disappeared, adding to the avalanche that thundered into the valley below.

Had they been saved?

Not by a long shot. The effort of the mules to pull the wagons free had increased their pace, and now it was propelling them down the mountain at breakneck speed. Brodie had half applied each wagon brake, but this was no longer enough. They were gaining momentum with each revolution of the giant wheels, causing the wagons to bounce and leap into the air while Brodie tried desperately to keep them on the narrow track.

How they managed to stay on course and upright was a mystery to Brodie. Maybe it was his skill or maybe it was just dumb luck. He couldn't say.

Or was it the sheer muscle of the mules to both pull and slow the giant procession enough for Brodie to maintain control? Or was it the God he had called upon? If so, which God? The God of the Spanish missionaries who had come to California, or the God of the Mormon pioneers who had passed this way to Utah? Or was it the God of the Timbisha Shoshone, the Great Spirit? Brodie had no idea. He wasn't a religious man who considered such thoughts. But if, by chance, it was the God of the Indians, why was a paleface worthy of such good grace?

Perhaps he should just thank them all.

When Brodie finally reached the valley floor, after being shot down the mountain pass as if from a cannon, it was with immense relief. And as the lathered mules finally slowed to a walk, it could be said that all were now safe. Or at least that's what Brodie thought because what happened next defies all reason. After such a harrowing, bone rattling and death-defying event, and while making a slow turn to bring the team to a halt, the front wheel on the second wagon sunk deep into soft sand causing it to tilt.

This was not a big deal. Brodie just needed to straighten up the mules and using a little more momentum, draw the wagon forward and back onto firmer ground. Of course, to make this correction, Brodie needed to maintain his position on top of the first wagon and keep a firm grip on the reins. Hardly a problem. After all, he'd been up there on that perch for the last 145 miles. So, it was beyond belief how he managed to fall off at this precise moment.

To Brodie it felt like he had been blown off by a sudden gust of wind. One that had come from nowhere. There could be no other explanation for it. Yet the mules didn't feel the force of any Mariah. One moment he was their master on high, the next he was tumbling through space to fall unceremoniously flat on his back in the sand with a thump.

The suddenness of this event took Brodie by complete surprise. In fact, it was difficult for him to accept what had happened as he squinted skywards into the bright blue just as a cloud cast its shadow across his face. Or at least he thought it was a cloud until he realized that it was the tall side of the second wagon blocking out the sun as it began to precariously lean over, while slowly continuing to edge by.

Brodie was now mesmerized by the hulk above him. With his feet facing towards the wagon, he saw the near wheels almost down to their hubs. Fine sand was spilling from the spokes like water from a paddle steamer. On glancing past his boots, he saw in horror that the wheels on the far side were no longer touching the ground. 'Good God,' he called out and began to frantically kick his feet in an effort to squirm and wriggle away from the impending doom.

It was too late.

The wagon had passed its tipping point, and as if in slow motion, the far wheels continued to lift into the air as the wagon began to roll onto its side. Brodie could see it coming, so he closed his eyes and screwed up his face in the grim hope that being crushed to death by a four-ton borax wagon wasn't going to hurt too much.

TWO

AN INNOCENT MAN
In Hell

He remained dead still, eyes screwed tight and his lips pursed taut. Just how long Brodie had held his breath he didn't know, but when he let it go the air came out with a rush. When brave enough to steal a glimpse at exactly what had happened, he did so by taking small, sneaky peeks. Above him was a grey expanse and as his eyes slowly focused, he began to make out what looked like a ceiling of rough, knotted wooden planks suspended some twelve inches above his nose. It was the side of the wagon, which blocked out the sun except for thin piercing lines of sunlight from between the timber slats. When he turned his head to each side, he could see the light patterns falling upon the sand and it exaggerated the expanse of this vast shallow tomb he now occupied.

When twisting his head to glance behind, he became totally disoriented. While he could clearly make out the two giant wheels lying on their sides, the hubs buried deep from the impact, his last recollection was of them to his front. Somehow his body had been turned around exactly 180 degrees. Had this occurred when he tried to scramble out of the way? If so, the memory of doing so had vanished. In fact, all he could recall was the spellbinding effect of watching death arrive in the form of a massive rolling wagon.

Brodie lifted his head until it touched the wagon and looked down towards his feet. The wooden ceiling disappeared on a descending angle into the dark. In fact, it looked as if his legs had been cut off below the knees. Tentatively, he moved the big toe in his right boot. With relief he felt it respond. He tried the left. It also moved. He went for a full wiggle and all those little piggies replied. 'Yippie, for that,' he said in a flat voice, 'at least you're still with me.' He bent his elbows and drew his hands up to his sides, then with a push on the palms he strained in an effort to slide himself free from this crypt beneath the wagon.

Nothing happened. His feet were firmly fixed.

'Come on,' he called out loud, 'let's go,' and pushed hard again.

Still nothing happened. It was as if his feet were cast in stone, yet he felt no pain or even discomfort.

'Don't do this to me, not now, it's been a long day.' Brodie was prone to talking to himself, it had come from years of working alone down a dark mine shaft, devoid of company and conversation. Not all of these discussions were just with himself, he'd debated much about life in general with his mules, especially when they showed the mildest interest. He'd even been known to have a heart-to-heart with the rocks, begging them to release their fortune in gold or silver. Maybe he was talking to those Gods again, the ones that got him down the mountain in one piece. But had they spared him from death only to trap him under this wagon?

As Brodie tried to figure out exactly what it was that now encased his feet, he also continued to grapple with what had exactly happened. The sequence of events as best he could recall, started with the second wagon tilting as the wheels sank deep into soft sand. Why this hadn't happened to the first wagon, the one he was on, was a mystery. Yet somehow, he was pitched over the side as if from a rolling boat on a stormy sea. The suddenness of it all had caught him by complete surprise. While confused, he could also clearly remember seeing the second wagon begin to roll onto its side in a gradual, almost gentle motion, with him lying on the ground beneath, watching the impending doom coming his way.

He dug the heels of his hands back into the dirt and strained again to release his feet, but nothing budged, not one inch. When moving his shoulders in preparation for another try, and what was now becoming a desperate situation, he felt a sharp jab to the small of his back. He lifted his left side for relief. Whatever it was, it was digging into him. In an effort to get to the cause of the problem he had to arch his back and edge his left hand beneath him by clawing at the ground. With some difficulty he finally felt the handle of his knife. It must have twisted on the belt during the fall. Slowly, he was able to ease it, bit by bit, from the leather scabbard. When free, he lifted his hand up and tilted his head to take a look. It was undamaged and none the worse for wear, unlike his back as the discomfort remained. He dropped the knife by his side in annoyance.

Again, he tried to move his feet, and again they remained firmly wedged. He even tried sliding further down under the wagon but that made no difference. He couldn't go forward, back or to either side. Yet, mysteriously his feet remained comfortable and the toes continued to wiggle on demand. Whatever was locked around his feet, showed no sign of letting go. This inability to comprehend exactly what was the cause of his incarceration made his predicament seem dreamlike.

Or was it, nightmare-like?

He dropped his head back onto the sand and the realization of this pickle was clear and stark. He had no way of getting out, no water, and no hope of rescue. The next borax wagon to come through this way was a week out. By that time, he'd be dead, and this was not going to be an easy death. It was only marginally better than being staked out by the Indians on an anthill as bait to draw the cavalry into an ambush. It was going to be miserable and long. The only consolation that came to mind was that there were no ants.

Out of the corner of his eye he thought he saw movement. He twisted his head to look through the gloom. Had it been sliding? 'Please, please not a rattler,' he pleaded and lifted his head to search the ground. He could see nothing as he slowly slid his hand sideways in search for the discarded knife.

When helplessly trapped with nothing more than your own thoughts and facing a dim yet certain future, the mind tends to wander, and Brodie's was no different. As night fell and the heat cooled to a desert chill, his mind began to drift back and slowly cascade through the years. Regrets and concerns seemed to take on a new and enlightened context. Exactly what was conscious thought drifting into unconscious dreams he couldn't tell, but all seemed to hold to a common thread of being imprisoned.

The light of the following day brought with it thirst. Brodie was used to discomfort and surviving on little water. It was often the one commodity as precious as gold on a mountain mine site. But no one could last for long without any water and that included the mules. They needed regular watering and were now becoming distressed. Still shackled to the first wagon, they were also trapped just like him. To now hear their calls of anguish and not be able to attend to their needs was to listen to the innocent being tortured. This affected Brodie deeply. It was his responsibility to care for his mules and he had failed.

By the following day it had driven him to contemplate the unthinkable.

If he used the knife to slit his wrists, he would be unconscious in minutes and dead within the hour. But to do so, just to relieve his suffering while leaving his twenty mules to theirs, was the act of a coward and for all Brodie's faults, cowardice had never been one of them. He used to say to his mules when times were tough, just remember, things are never as good as you think, and never as bad. But really, how much worse could this get and why? He could only assume that somewhere along the line he had caused great offence to the Gods and now he was paying his dues a thousand-fold.

When he heard the familiar sound of hoofs thumping upon the sand he wondered if some of the mules had managed to free themselves. Even if they had, then what? If the water tank was still upright, they wouldn't be able to drink from it. The tap would be locked off tight. When the thumping came closer, behind him, he twisted his head with difficulty and thought he saw white fetlocks. All his mules were black. Maybe he was suffering from delusions or losing his vision. He closed his eyes.

The voice that spoke was soft and close. 'You look to be in some difficulty, my son.'

Brodie opened his eyes with a start. The face leaning over him was Indian and chalky white. It was

such an unexpected sight that he had trouble focus-
ing his eyes and had to keep blinking. Slowly, as his
sight adjusted, he could see the angular nose and
the high cheekbones of a noble face. Plaits with tufts
of colourful feathers intertwined at intervals hung
down to brush Brodie's face. He swallowed hard and
croaked, 'Water.'

'Don't carry it,' said the Indian without much concern. 'I have no need. I carry a watch though, a gold
one on a chain. I can tell you the time, if you want.'
He produced the timepiece and dangled it in front of
Brodie's face. 'It's later than you think.'

Brodie just said, 'Feet.'

The Indian turned his head to look down at
Brodie's feet. 'You look stuck.'

'Can't move my feet. Jammed. Can you see?'

The Indian lowered his head a little and the feathers touched Brodie's face again. 'No, too dark.'

Brodie lifted his arm with difficulty to gesture.
'The mules. Water the mules for me.'

'You need saving,' said the Indian.

'The mules first.'

The Indian's nose was now so close that he could
hear him softly breathing in. He was smelling Brodie.

'Tanka,' he said. 'Tanka is nearby, I think he will
come this time.'

'With water?' wheezed Brodie.

'Much better. To bestow the Divine Wind upon
you. But only if you are worthy to serve.'

Brodie watched as the white face began to depart from his view. The Indian was crawling back out from under the wagon. He tried to reach up, to grab him, but he was far too slow. Frantically he called in stilted words, 'Free my feet, shovel, on one of the wagons. Dig me free.'

He didn't receive a reply.

All he heard were the sounds of thumping hooves as the Indian upon his horse rode away into the distance.

Brodie was not an emotional man nor one to dwell on what might or might not have been. He accepted life as it was handed to him and had made the best of it. But at that precise moment he just wished that it would end. How long he'd been in this tomb he didn't know. Was it three days or four, maybe even five? Or was it a lifetime? Whatever it was, he now knew for certain that this was a punishment, and by its very nature the worst kind – the one where the accused is yet to know of the charge against him. What was the crime and the evidence of his guilt?

In his heart Brodie knew he was an innocent man. 'Take me now,' he whispered. 'Hell can't be worse.'

THREE

SERENITY
Whirlwind

When Brodie opened his eyes, the sky was a cloudless beautiful blue, the temperature wonderfully cool and a soft sweet breeze caressed his face. For a moment he forgot where he was and of his dire situation. He guessed that he was slowly coming out of a dream and closed his eyes in the hope that he could make it last just a little longer.

During the war, he'd seen battlefield casualties, men with missing limbs and in great pain, who entered a state of complete serenity just before death. Was this now happening to him? Without a thought he lifted his knee, drew up his foot and wriggled all the toes in his boot. It felt good, so he did the same to his other leg, and that's when he reopened his eyes, looked around, and sat bolt upright.

The only sound was of the light breeze as it passed his ears, as if in a quiet caress. Before him was a borax wagon lying on its side. It was the second wagon, the first was still upright and the mules were all hitched and standing quietly, ready and waiting to go. To his left was the water tank, it too was upright.

He pushed himself up onto his feet and felt a little unsteady and lightheaded, forcing him to go back down onto his haunches and take in some deep breaths. 'What the hell is going on?' he asked himself, before counting to three, picking up his hat, which lay a couple of feet away, to stand again. One of the mules called, but it was not in distress, more like, come on, we're rigged to go.

Brodie made his way over to the team, having to steady himself on the side of the first wagon from a stagger on shaky legs. He then began to attend to the mules by slowly patting the nearside one of each pair, while checking their harness and appearance. All were in top health and the hitches in good order. He did the same again down the other side of the team, checking and rubbing a hand over the closest mule. He then made his way to the first borax wagon, which stood proud and was in sound condition.

The second wagon lay on its side and unhooked from the first wagon. This confused Brodie as on closer inspection the yoke was unattached and the kingpin lay on the ground. It was the same situation for the water wagon, as it too was unlatched with its kingpin removed. He rapped on the side of the tank with his knuckles, it was still half filled, and when he placed his hand on the riveted metal plate, it was delightfully cool.

Brodie did not stop to ponder this mystery for long. A sense of light-headed euphoria mixed with a burning desire to get the hell out of there saw him unshackle the team, walk them around on the chain to the side of the second wagon, jury-rig a spider to the upturned wheels and commence to right the wagon. It was done with ease by a master and his team working as one. He then led the mules around to the water wagon, hooked up the canvas trough, filled it with water and brought each pair forward to drink. All took water but none were in any hurry to quench a thirst. When Brodie drank, the water tasted sweet but like the mules he really didn't feel that thirsty.

On re-hitching the team and reconnecting the wagons, he walked back around to the other side of the train to mount the first wagon. As he stepped up onto the hub and then on to the top of the rim, he looked back down to where the second wagon had rolled onto its side. Lying on the ground was his knife. He got back down and slowly walked over to where it rested. On kneeling to pick it up, Brodie could see the marks on the ground. It showed scrapings in the shape of a man, and close to his knee was a small colourful tuft of feathers. He picked it up and examined it carefully as the wind blew, making the tiny feathers flutter. He placed the little plumage in the top pocket of his shirt, picked up his knife and returned it to the scabbard on his belt.

Just as he was ready to remount, a small whirl-wind kicked up dust over to his right. He watched as it started to spin. A rattlesnake slid away to safety as the wind danced towards the second wagon, and in a flurry sucked up the dirt where his knife had lay and sent it towards the heavens, leaving a smooth unblemished surface behind.

Brodie pulled on the brim of his hat to hold it tight against the wind and mounted the first wagon. As soon as he was on top, he gripped the reins and with-out looking back, yelled, 'Yee-haw,' and twenty mules pulled as one to roll the wagons on their way.

FOUR

WHITE HORSE

A Lost Week

When Brodie pulled the team into Furnace Creek, he was met by Billy May, who gave the shout, 'We'd just about given you up for dead.' Billy was a fellow miner turned muleskinner who also hauled borax to the Mojave railhead. Before Brodie could answer, Billy added, 'Where's Pat?'

Brodie got down off the wagon before saying, 'Pat's passed on, Bill.'

'Pat! Our Pat?

Brodie nodded. 'Doc at Mojave said his heart gave up on him. Happened in his sleep.'

'And Steve didn't stay to help you get the wagons back?'

'Steve had already left. He got on the Southern for Los Angeles the day before, just as he'd planned.

Even if he'd hadn't, I wouldn't have asked him to stay. He had a boat to catch. All his plans were in place.'

'And you brought the train back on your own?' said Billy in amazement.

Brodie just nodded and rubbed the small of his back that was a little tender.

'You oughta not done that Bob, too dangerous.'

'You're telling me,' said Brodie, 'I had a hell of a time of it.'

Billy was sporting a broad smile. It was how he saw life, always on the sunny side. 'Well, at least you got back here safe and sound, and none the worse for wear.'

'Not too sure about that, Billy. I had a mishap just below the Skidoo.'

Brodie had commenced to unhitch the mules and Billy began to give him a hand, saying, 'I think we're going to have to close that pass. It was bad the last time I went through.'

'Worse now, but it was off the pass that I took a tumble. The number two wagon rolled on me in soft sand.'

'Soft sand there? Odd. Have to look out for that,' noted Billy. 'Just as well it wasn't the lead wagon, it could have thrown you off and rolled on top of you.' His eyes grinned with his smile.

Brodie pressed his lips tight as if to stop from saying something silly, before muttering, 'Yeah, just as well.'

'I can now see why you're a week late.'

Brodie's head jerked a little. 'A week!'

'To the day,' said Billy.

'Can't be. Not a week.'

'Easy to lose a week if you couldn't get away from Mojave on time due to Pat's passing and had to make repairs on the road. All chews up the clock, don't it? I'd say you could lose a week easy.'

Brodie had left only two days late from the rail-head and made most of that time up before he got to the Skidoo. 'There was no damage to repair at all,' he said. 'Just kind of rolled over on its own, sort of easy like.'

Billy was now a little confused and it showed when he pushed his hat back and scratched his head.

Brodie kept unharnessing the mules in silence before he asked, 'Bill, what do you know of the Timbisha?'

Bill kept scratching. 'Not much to know, is there?'

'I'm not too sure about that, anymore. I met one on the way. Or at least I think I met one.'

'An Indian? Where?'

'The Skidoo.'

'That would have to be Timbisha. No other tribe goes near there that I know of.'

'What did he want?' asked Billy.

Brodie gave the question some thought before answering, his fingers continuing to work the leather straps with speed. 'Hard to say. I don't think he wanted anything.'

Billy nodded his head in agreement. 'Yeah, hard to know when they can't speak our language.'

'No, he could speak English fine. I think most of them can. It's just us who only know the odd Indian word or two.'

Billy didn't know what to make of Brodie's comment. Why would anyone want to learn an Indian language? he thought.

'Might go over and have a talk to them tomorrow. See if I can track him down.'

'To do what?' asked Billy.

'Don't know exactly,' said Brodie. 'I've just been doing a little figuring that's all and think it might be time to move on.'

This took Billy by surprise. 'Move on? You going back to mining?'

'No, that's behind me, too.'

Billy was now confused and maybe you are too, because obscure conversations often occur between two men when one won't actually say what it is that is bothering him. In seeking some kind of clarification, Billy asked, 'So, what are you going to do?'

'Still thinking about that,' said Brodie. At the moment, I'm just happy to be alive and out in the sun.'

Billy slapped Brodie's upper arm. 'Good to hear, and good to see you back. Not like you to come in late, ever. We were thinking that we might have to send out a search party in the next week or two.'

'That would have helped,' said Brodie with a thin smile and reached into his shirt pocket to pull out the tuft of feathers. 'Ever seen one of these before?'

Billy lent over to take a closer look as Brodie held it up at eye level. 'Pretty. But no, never seen anything like that. Timbisha?'

'I'm guessing,' said Brodie.

'Smells good,' said Billy May sniffing.

'Does it?' Brodie took a sniff. 'I can't smell nothing.'

Billy took a deep breath in through the nose and frowned. He tried again, his nose getting closer to Brodie. 'It's you. The smell is coming from you.'

Brodie lifted an arm to sniff. 'I can't smell a thing, but who can when you've been on the trail. I'll wash up later.'

'No,' said Billy, 'it's nothing bad.' He kept sniffing. 'It smells like almonds. You know, the baked kind. Roasted. Have you been eating almonds?'

'Roasted almonds?' said Brodie shaking his head a little. 'No.'

'Smells OK. Must've brushed up against something.'

'Can't think what,' said Brodie. 'Maybe it's come from the mules.'

'Mules?' said Billy. 'Never smelt no mule that was like almonds. No, it's definitely not them. It's you.'

* * *

The Timbisha Shoshone camp was down past the Chinese camp, some three miles from the Furnace

Creek Harmony works. Brodie took his time when walking there the following morning, using the early solitude to sort through his thoughts. He'd done a lot of sorting of late, especially on the twenty-mile haul back from the Skidoo Pass immediately after his miraculous revival. Or should we say resurrection by the Gods?

The only logical conclusion that he could draw about what had actually happened went something like this: Due to a sudden tilt of the wagon he'd been thrown to the ground and knocked out, or at least left dazed. His final sight on the way down, while tumbling through the air, or crawling out of the way, was of the second wagon heading in his direction. Fortunately, somehow, the wagon just missed him as it landed on its side, and while lying unconscious, he had experienced a vivid and delusionary dream of being trapped. On waking, a little time later, the reality and the dream became confused as to what had actually happened, leaving him disoriented to his surroundings.

Each time Brodie repeated this little story to himself, it seemed to make more sense – except for the crawling out of the way first before he passed out. However, now was not the time to get too caught up in the detail. After all, dreams happened. Real intense dreams at times.

He was used to dreams. He'd had lots of troubling dreams just after the war and they were all similar with one common theme. He would find himself being chased through the woods by the Feds, after somehow losing his rifle in the process. Now in fear of being caught, he would suddenly fall into a big, deep, dark hole full of more Feds and have to fight his way out with his bare hands.

Nothing like that had ever happened to him in real life. It was just a disturbing dream. And that's why Brodie believed that dreams from the dead of the night were best not given credence during the light of day. Besides, what good would it do anyway? Some things in life could never be fully explained. Eventually, the dreams from the war settled down, except for the odd one or two that just turned up unexpectedly. Maybe getting caught under the wagon was just like being chased and falling into a hole? It was all in the head. But if it was, this had been the most realistic of dreams he'd ever had in his life and one that he didn't wish to repeat. Perhaps it was the sort of dream that occurred when knocked out as opposed to just nodding off.

Of course, none of this explained the finding of his knife under the wagon or the tuft of feathers. Or the marks upon the ground of where he had lay on his back. These were beyond mysterious. As was the visit from the old white-faced Indian. Even Brodie knew that sweeping away such particulars into the realm of dreams was asking a bit much, and that's why he trudged on towards the Indian camp.

The glory of the Valley on this morning was on display. She had lifted her skirt as if to tease with the beauty of an ankle. Brodie had been here long enough to see her do this from time to time. It was not an everyday occurrence as the mild seasons were short and fickle, but today was a clear sky with a soft pleasant breeze. Actually, the weather since the odd events at the Skidoo had been exceptionally pleasant.

Brodie filled his lungs with a deep breath in appreciation of being alive and he felt good, only to have his mind drift back to what had actually happened below the Skidoo Pass, and that other pressing question. How could he possibly lose one whole week out of his life?

When Brodie was told of the missing week, he just thought Billy had got the dates wrong. But when he asked around everyone gave him the same answer that he was exactly one week late. He thought that maybe Billy had set him up to have his leg pulled and all were in on it. So, he asked Frenchie, even though Billy was no trickster, and Daunet, a man of no nonsense, and they both confirmed the date. One week had somehow been lost. This rattled Brodie. Clearly, he hadn't lay out there on his back unconscious for all that time. If he had, he and the mules would have died of thirst.

The visit to the Indian camp was going to be a long shot, he knew that, but he had to try. He had to ask about the old Indian with the white face. The one who had called on Tanka, whoever he was.

When Brodie arrived on the edge of the village with its scruffy grass houses, he stood quietly and waited to be seen. The children, who were playing, saw him, stopped and looked. So, he waved. They waved back and were joined by a woman. He waved again and she acknowledged with a nod then left, returning with one of the men. Brodie stretched out his arms, palms turned towards the man and fingers splayed. Why he did this he wasn't sure, other than to show that he came in peace.

He was beckoned forward.

'I met a man. I think from here. I would like to meet him again,' called Brodie before adding. 'I think he helped me, but I'm not sure. If it was him, I'd like to thank him.'

The man, younger than Brodie, gestured for him to advance into the camp. The children followed and stayed with Brodie until an older man came to join him with most of the tribe in tow. Brodie went to explain again, but before he could get a word out, the older man said softly and calmly in good English. 'If you had met anyone from here, they would have told us of meeting and helping you.'

'If he isn't from here, maybe you might still know of him. He had a white-painted face. Very white, like chalk.'

The old Indian shook his head.

'He had plaits, and—' Brodie pulled the tuft of feathers from his shirt pocket and handed it over. 'I believe this is his.'

The older Indian shook his head again and handed it back.

'Well, thank you,' said Brodie, replacing the feathers in his pocket.

On turning to leave he realized that he was now surrounded by most of the camp. He turned back. 'This man with the white face said a word to me. It may be Timbisha. He said, Tanka.'

The crowd around him let out a little gasp.

The old Indian looked at the ground, then across to the younger man who Brodie had first spoken to, and tilted his head. He nodded in response and quickly disappeared through the throng that were now chatting to themselves in low tones.

When the younger man returned, he escorted a very old woman. She slowly made her way towards Brodie and took a good look through squinting eyes before saying, 'Tosa Kapayu.'

Brodie turned to the younger Indian and shrugged.

'It is the name of her husband. It means White Horse.'

'Can I talk to him?' asked Brodie.

'No,' said the older Indian. 'Tosa Kapayu has been dead for many years. I was a young man when he passed.'

The old woman was staring intently at Brodie and it was a little unnerving.

Not knowing what to do, he pulled the tuff of feathers back out of his pocket.

Her eyes lit up immediately and she clasped her hands around his. 'Tosa Kapayu,' she repeated and slowly lent in to sniff Brodie's cheeks on each side, nodding her head as she began to mumble a chant.

Brodie once again turned to the older Indian. 'I don't understand.'

'She is telling everyone that her husband Tosa Kapayu has called on Tanka, the Great Spirit, to anoint you with the Divine Wind.'

'What does that mean?' he asked.

The noise of those around Brodie was getting louder as the tribe had joined with the woman in her chant.

'It means you are a chosen one. You now take her husband's place. He will no longer be left to wander the wastelands. He may now go to a tranquil place of peace.'

'Take his place, how?' asked Brodie.

The man spoke to the woman and she seemed to be providing advice. Finally, he said, 'Your life has not been lived. You must be guided by the Divine Wind to help and care for those who are important to you. If not, you will become lost to wander in the wastclands.'

'And how will I be guided by this Divine Wind?' mumbled Brodie under his breath.

The woman sniffed the air and in faultless English said, 'Follow your nose and your heart and you will be rewarded with riches beyond belief, beyond your dreams. However, you must serve and protect those you love and who love you, if you are to be worthy of such fortune.'

The chanting was now becoming very loud, yet it wasn't annoying or disturbing. In fact, to Brodie's ears, it felt as if they were cheering him on in a quest to live his life as guided by the Divine Wind.

FIVE

A SECOND CHANCE
Also, on the Road

Brodie broke the news to Bill May that same afternoon. He was leaving Death Valley, and it was for good.

The news of leaving for good certainly caught Billy by surprise as he asked, 'Where are you going?'

'Back to see my sisters in Frisco.'

'Why now after all these years?'

'They were important in my life.' Brodie wanted to add, 'and I never got to tell them,' but it sounded wet, so he left it out.

Then what?' asked Billy.

'Don't know for sure,' said Brodie. 'Might just follow…' He was going to say the wind, but instead said, 'my nose. I have some money. More than any other time in my life. I can do mule work. A little hauling. I'll find something. I'll survive.'

'If you can survive this place, you can survive any place. How many sisters do you have?'

'Four.'

'When did you last see 'em?'

'Before the war,' said Brodie.

Billy pushed his hat back and gave his itchy scalp a scratch, which he was fond of doing when trying to figure out exactly what was going on. 'That long. Close to twenty-five years. Will they remember you?'

'They'll remember. Women do. I was the youngest. They brought me up. They'll have kept the memories.'

'Like when they wiped your backside as a young 'un', eh?'

'Yeah, something like that,' said Brodie with a touch of annoyance. 'But they don't need reminding of that from me.'

'No, of course,' said a contrite Billy. 'Just ribbing that's all. You gonna write first?'

Brodie shook his head. 'No need. I reckon I'll beat any mail I send from here.' He looked over at the mules in the corral. 'I'll need two to take with me.'

'Any in particular?'

'Yeah, I'd like Smith and Jones.'

'Well, if you pick 'em out, you can have 'em. All look the same to me. The company charge is seventy-five each, but I'll see what I can do 'cos that is way overpriced.'

41

'I'm going to have to sup-up from the store.'

Billy pulled a face of mild discomfort. 'That'll cost you. Why not just do another run? You'll have to go out through Mojave anyway. Save you some. Save you a lot. Won't need any mules either, you can just jump the Southern Pacific up to Frisco from there.'

Brodie knew it was the smart thing to do, but he wanted different. He didn't want to do the Mojave route one more time, and if he did, Harmony would say, why not do one more after that and they could be real persuasive, especially if they paid in advance. Something deep inside Brodie said, make a clean break. 'No, I'm going to take my time and head down to the San Joaquin and pick up the Southern out of Bakersfield.'

'It's longer than to Mojave.'

'A bit.'

'Forty-mile more.'

'I'm in no hurry. It will give me one last look at the mountains, because I won't be coming back, ever.'

Bill nodded his acceptance of the situation. 'But are you sure you want to go to San Francisco, it's a dangerous place. Had an earthquake in '68. I know, I was there. Nearly had a house fall on me. I was just walking down the sidewalk minding my own business and down it come.'

'Yeah, but that was a good while ago. Might not happen again for a thousand years or more.'

'You want to take that risk?'

'If a house falls on me, I'll well and truly know it's my time.' Brodie glanced over at the transport yard.

'And you never know, a borax wagon might fall on top of you one day, Billy. This is also a dangerous business.'

Billy laughed out loud, 'It might be dangerous, but it pays well,' before asking more seriously, 'When will you leave?'

'Next day or two. I don't have much to pack.'

Bill put out his hand.

'I'll see you before I go,' said Brodie, balking at taking his shake.

'I know,' said Bill. 'But you've been a good partner Robert Brodie and I thank you for that. If there is any help needed between then and now, you just holler.'

'I will,' said Brodie as he finally grasped Bill's hand, but it was done with no enthusiasm. It was as if the realization of his decision to leave had now been sealed and there was no turning back.

* * *

Brodie left on foot three days later leading two mules, Sergeant Smith and Corporal Jones. Each were loaded with enough supplies for two weeks, a month in all, even six weeks on reduced rations. Not that Brodie planned to be on the road for that long. The distance from Furnace Creek to the Southern Pacific rail station at Bakersfield was just over two hundred miles and it could be done in two weeks, all things being equal. However, Brodie was in no hurry. He was neither going to press himself or the mules. If it took two and half or even three weeks that would be fine – and he wasn't going lean either, like he had so many times in his life. He would eat well, and he knew where the water was and would stop over wherever necessary.

The personal items he took with him were few. One spare pair of Strauss blue rivet waist overalls; two spare, long-sleeved, white, collarless, cotton work shirts with pockets; one lightweight wool-weave jacket, mostly draped over one of the pack mules and worn at night when chilly; two linen bandanas, one red and one blue; one pair of Jefferson boots always worn; and, one Stetson-brand cavalry hat that never seemed to leave his head. He even slept under it, tilted low over his eyes.

He preferred a belt to braces and that was where he hung his knife. His rifle was a Model 73 lever-action Winchester and his pistol a single-action Army Colt with its own belt and holster. Both weapons chambered different calibre ammunition; the rifle .44 and the pistol .45. The quantity of ammunition he carried was less than fifty rounds combined, which came in boxes of twelve that had been purchased in Mojave two years prior. His musketry skills from Army days as a Confederate held him in good stead if needed, but they had rarely been used over the years, other than to chase off the odd hound snooping around his mining claim. Both his rifle and pistol were well maintained and lightly oiled weekly from force of habit.

He owned no homely goods nor chattels except for cooking and eating implements and a burnt black coffee pot. Of course, there was also his pick and shovel. These last two items he had acquired some twenty years before. The handles of both were dark and smooth from where his hands had gripped them daily, right up until the time he left mining to become a muleskinner. These accoutrements were part of Brodie, like his boots and hat. He would have taken them with him on the borax drives, except the company provided all the mechanical necessities, which were stowed in the toolboxes of each wagon. When the mules were loaded up, Smith took the pick and Jones the shovel. Both implements were roped to the outside of the canvas-covered saddle-packs for easy access if needed to dig or pick at a rock or two, in a final chance of finding that elusive fortune.

Brodie's rather casual approach to the time he would take for this journey was unusual. He tended to grit things out, get 'em done, and move on. But circumstances had changed, and it had all happened in his head, and rather quickly. He'd mulled over what the old Indian woman had said to him and it had more than a ring of truth to it. Not the following of the Divine Wind so much, which he guessed was some sort of tribal folklore, but the need to serve and protect those he loved. That, of course, had to be his family, his sisters, who had nurtured him into manhood. As for being rewarded with a fortune of riches beyond belief, beyond his dreams, he presumed that this was about having a fortunate life, one free from the guilt of being so careless towards his family in the past, especially his mother.

Her death had left him with feelings of shame that popped into his head, unannounced, from time to time. His had been a solitary life and often when digging deep in a shaft, he would think of his youth, his sisters and in particular his mother, Minnie. He had rarely written and when he did, his words were brief and lacked the care and appreciation deserved from an only son. If he was honest with himself, which Brodie could be from time to time, he had spent the last twenty years preoccupied with the sole endeavour of striking it rich.

Now he wondered, was it not just folly, but also selfishness?

These thoughts that rattled around inside his head were somewhat uncomfortable, and only got worse when he speculated as to what he would have done had he struck it rich. Say he'd found the motherlode, a seam of pure gold and become an overnight millionaire. What then? Live the high life? Sail the seven seas as a first-class passenger? Travel to exotic lands? Buy the biggest house on the hill? Such a line of enquiry made him feel uneasy as he tramped towards the San Joaquin Valley and in turn, led to another vexing question. Why hadn't he considered any of this long before now?

Had it not been for the intervention of strange events, he would not be on this journey. A journey that now felt like destiny. If you were hearing this story from a Biblical man, he might tell you that it was Brodie's fall on the road to Damascus, rather than from a borax wagon below the Skidoo Pass.

Brodie, after so long, had been knocked into consciousness.

He was seeing the world around him differently. The mountains looked prettier, the air smelt fresher, and there was an unusual lightness under each of his steps. He was, after all, just grateful to be alive, and that was understandable. It was only a week ago that he thought his life was going to come to a nasty end. A life that had been lived the same way, each day, every day, over and over again, without change, without question. What Brodie didn't really appreciate was that he had accidently been reborn. The big question that followed, however, was what did he plan to do with this resurrection?

Just drift?

Or was he actually going to put some effort into living a better life – whatever that may really mean? Hopefully, that Divine Wind had the answer because Brodie sure didn't.

* * *

Also, on the road at that time were other travellers. Like the Klutters, a father and daughter from San Bernardino who had been willed a mining claim from a recently departed relative – a man who had worked the diggings in and around the Skidoo some decade or two before. Their dream was to prize enough precious metal out of the earth for the purchase of an orange orchard in Crafton. They had even set their eyes on a particular property, one in the valley with mature trees that were already fruiting with good yields.

Then there were the Olsens from Beaumont, a Mormon family consisting of father Joseph, wife Ada, daughter Hannah and baby brother Eden, heading for Salt Lake City to settle down peacefully amongst their brethren.

And on horseback were four men who had come north over the border near Tijuana after the sale of stolen horses to the Mexican Army. Jake Bass, Wes Gary, Chad Thompson and Leland Gill were looking for any opportunity to fill their pockets, and if it meant killing, that didn't much matter. Jake shot dead a travelling salesman near La Mesa on a whim, and at Barstow the four robbed the general store, firing shots, before starting the journey east towards Flagstaff. They planned to hold up the post office on information that the wages for the workers of the Mars Hill Lumber Company were delivered there on the second Tuesday of each month.

All these travellers were a distance away from Brodie, but they were heading in his direction as they journeyed towards Death Valley. Would their paths cross? Who knew? The Timbisha Shoshone may have seen Brodie as a chosen one, but the Divine Wind had not bestowed much in the way of providence upon him. In fact, he had all but dismissed the Divine Wind as nothing more than some mythical belief as he plodded on, putting one foot in front of the other, in the ignorant bliss that things would just sort themselves out. Why not? They had in the past, somehow.

SIX

FELLOW TRAVELLERS

Dreams

Brodie had always done more walking than riding. He walked with his mules as they pulled the mining carts of oar. He preferred to walk with them on most of the borax drives and leave others to ride the wagons or a mule. It allowed him to check harnesses and for sore or lame legs, and it allowed him to talk to each and every mule. He could urge them on up a hill, slow them down a slope, or just plain chat with them. He knew it was an odd habit and one not to be done under the public gaze. It could look a bit odd, to say the least – talking to the animals.

Fortunately, he wasn't in a deep conservation with his mules when he met Miss Chastity Klutter. Had he been, he would have felt rather embarrassed as some idiosyncrasies are best kept to oneself. It was late in the day and she had been hidden from view, just where the track turned a corner near a large rock.

When, still unseen, she called out in a loud voice, 'My oh my.'

Brodie was caught by complete surprise. He thought it was a voice from the heavens, until he saw her standing in the middle of the road. It was as if she had appeared from nowhere. He snatched the hat from his head in well-mannered respect and stopped dead in his tracks.

Chasity, on seeing Brodie, immediately exclaimed, 'Oh Lord, where did you come from? Almost startled the living daylights out of me.'

Brodie tripping over his words, said, 'I didn't. Didn't mean to—' before making the observation. 'But you are standing in the way and acting as an obstacle.'

Chastity's eyes widened in response. 'I am doing no such thing. I was just doing my breathing exercises and admiring the view. We have seen no one on this road for well over a week.' A hand was confidently thrust forward in Brodie's direction by way of introduction. 'Chastity Klutter, and you are?'

Brodie was still coming to grips at seeing a young woman in such an unexpected place. This was the middle of nowhere, surrounded by dirt, and here she was so clean and neat, dressed in blue with a white apron and white bonnet, right there standing before him. He only got to see a woman or two in Mojave each month and they never spoke to him or him to them. And he never really got to actually look at them up this close. 'Brodie,' he said hesitantly and went to introduce his mules by name but stopped short, just saying, 'These are my mules.'

'I gathered that, Mr Brodie,' said Chastity. 'I take it that you are on your own, though?' Her hand was still extended.

'I am,' confirmed Brodie as Jones let out a sharp call of rebuke for not being introduced by name. 'Along with my mules, both of them, together.' Then he added as if in contrition, 'three of us in all,' while gingerly stepping forward to extend his hand. The touch was brief. Not because Chastity wanted it so, but because Brodie felt so ill at ease. She was so near that he was able to smell her scent of lavender.

'We are camping here for the night,' announced Chastity Klutter. 'Would you care to join us?'

It was such a forward and sudden invitation that Brodie didn't know quite what to say other than some drawn out, 'Arrrs,' that Chastity took to be yes.

'Good,' she said, 'I will tell my father.'

Brodie met Mr Klutter near their wagon. He came out from behind some rocks where he had been relieving himself, wiping both hands down the sides of his dark green pants and saying, 'I thought I heard voices.' He extended a hand. 'Frederick Klutter of San Bernardino and soon to be of Death Valley.'

He took Mr Klutter's hand. 'Robert Brodie.'

'And where are you from, Robert?'

'Furnace Creek.'

'Oh, Death Valley.'

Brodie confirmed with a nod.

'Now tell me, does Furnace Creek live up to its name? Does it get as hot as a furnace?'

'It does,' said Brodie. 'But that's not how it got its name. A furnace was built there for mining. Borax is refined there.'

'Oh, I didn't know that. How interesting.'

'Or is all that fiery heat just talk?' asked Chastity. 'Today is such a beautiful day.'

Brodie agreed with another nod. It was indeed a beautiful day, but that just showed how wickedly deceptive this place could be. The pioneers who named the Valley in the winter of '49 to '50 were only slightly touched by its savagery. Yet the name they gave was more than appropriate. The bones of men lay where they had fallen and remained untouched for years. It was an isolated and desolate place, and one not to be taken lightly.

Brodie had managed to settle and regain a little self-assurance. 'It has its dispositions,' he said before asking, 'What puts you on this road?'

Chastity hesitated as if not wanting to answer. 'Would you like a slice of orange? It is still plump. It comes from the church orchard. A charitable donation of one dozen from our fellow parishioners.'

The subject had been changed in an instant from why they were on this journey to the offer of an orange, and all in a blink of an eye. Brodie had not tasted any fresh fruit in months. The cost of an orange, even in Mojave, was exorbitant, and now he was being offered a slice. But he would need to provide something in return. All he had was salted pork or beef, beans and coffee. So, politely, he refrained. 'Thank you but no thank you.'

'I insist.'

'I have nothing to return in kind,' he said.

'I suggest you have Mr Brodie,' said Mr Klutter. Maybe, you could tell of your experiences in the Valley. You look like you have been there some little while.'

'Twenty years,' said Brodie.

'A wealth of knowledge awaits us, Chastity. Provided we ask the right questions. And all for the price of a slice of orange. Now that will be payment enough.' Mr Klutter smiled at his daughter.

She smiled in agreement. 'Mr Brodie, would you wish to also sup with us?'

Brodie did sup with the Klutters and he contributed pinto beans to the community stew pot and coffee beans to the grinder for the coffee pot. The orange slice was eaten before the meal. Brodie delighted in the smell of the rind as his teeth scraped away the flesh. It was more than a small pleasure. It was an unexpected delight, as was the feeling of ease that came upon him as they chattered and ate.

Mr Klutter had many questions. He was keen to learn about the ways and seasons of Death Valley, the tracks and passes, and the availability of water other than the marked wells. When the coffee was almost exhausted, he asked, 'Mr Brodie, I noticed your pick and shovel. Are you a miner by chance?'

Brodie shook his head. 'Was once. Mined for nearly eighteen years.'

Mr Klutter couldn't hide his keen interest. 'Really, that long, and all in Death Valley?

Brodie nodded and sipped from his tin cup.

'May I ask of the skills and techniques required for such a venture?'

Chastity's eyes were fixed upon Brodie.

'Other than a strong back and thick head?' Brodie smiled at his own humour.

Mr Klutter also laughed, his daughter didn't. 'Just say myself and my daughter would wish to become miners for a day. Would we do well?'

It was a question that hinted towards an answer wanted but not directly requested, so he just said, 'Depends.'

Silence followed and it gave away the Klutters' intentions.

Brodie broke the silence by saying, 'You're not planning on going to Death Valley to mine, are you?'

Frederick Klutter started to say, 'Oh, no—'

He was cut short by his daughter who said, 'Why not? We are strong, fit and healthy. It can't be that difficult.'

Brodie gently scoffed and put his lips back to the cup and drank.

This seemed to infuriate Chastity Klutter, who questioned via a high-pitched false laugh, 'Mr Brodie does not agree with my proposition?'

Brodie couldn't get over how much she sounded like his sister Beth, who was renowned for her forthright way of calling out hogwash with humour. 'No, he does not,' said Brodie with the warmest smile he could muster.

'And why is that?' Chastity's chin was pointing at Brodie in defiance.

'It is hard, dirty work and crawling around a dark mineshaft on your hands and knees with a pick in your hands and sucking up dust into your lungs is no place for an elegant lady like yourself, nor a refined gentleman like you, sir.'

Chastity's mouth had opened ready to rebuke Brodie, but she now paused and her brow wrinkled under her white day cap. She was trying to figure if she had just been chastised or complimented. She really wasn't sure.

Brodie went back to sipping his coffee.

Mr Klutter sucked in a quick breath that swelled his waistcoat and jiggled the watch chain across his girth, before letting it out to say, rather quietly, 'We have inherited a mining claim. We believe it may be a path to our fortune.'

Once upon a time, telling a total stranger, especially while on the road, that you held a mining claim would have been most foolish. If stolen, it provided nine-tenths of the law to work that claim and own what it yielded. The Klutters didn't know Brodie from Adam and he *was* armed, but by 1885 any self-respecting shyster knew that a Death Valley mining claim was no road to riches, if it ever had been in the first place.

There had been no bonanza here like the northern California rush of '49. The gold that came out of the Valley had not been washed into streams so that it could be panned or sifted from the gravel of river beds. What had been found in this desolate place was often no more than a thin and intermittent vein that twisted and turned as it burrowed deep back in to the mountains. To get any worthwhile return, massive amounts of spoil had to be shifted by hand and few had either the determination or tenacity to persist for the months and years required.

However, the point of interest that now intrigued Brodie was the thought that maybe they trusted him. If so, was it from innocent naivety or the good judgement of his character? He decided to put it to the test. 'Where exactly is your claim?' he asked.

'Around a location known as the Skidoo. Do you know it?'

'I do,' said Brodie and threw the dregs of his coffee onto the fire.

'Is it good gold mining country?'

'I would have to see the precise location of your claim.'

'We couldn't show you that,' cut in Chastity.

'Why not?'

'You might—'

Brodie smiled and finished the sentence for her, 'steal it from you?'

'No, no,' said Mr Klutter.

The look on Chastity's face said different.

Brodie liked her caution. Trust should never be given out lightly. 'I don't need to see it,' he said. 'I know the Skidoo well and in my experience success would be difficult.'

'What about silver then?'

'Even less.'

The Klutters went quiet before Mr Klutter asked, 'Then what do we need to gain success?'

'Apart from luck?'

'Yes, apart from luck,' said Mr Klutter.

'More luck.' Brodie gave a little laugh.

This light-hearted attempt at mirth didn't seem to humour Chastity, who said, 'In all things a person must follow their dreams.'

Brodie didn't want to get into an argument. He had not had a conversation like this with a young woman in such a long time. She was confident and forthright, and it did so remind him of his sisters who were all smart, independent and outspoken. And of course, there was also her pleasing looks, which he could not deny. She had fresh skin, a neat figure, a pretty face with clear blue eyes that were absolutely captivating. The total effect was one of–

He couldn't find the right word, but you and I can. She was bewitching and Brodie was enchanted.

'Dreams,' he repeated.

'Yes,' said Chastity. 'Dreams,' before announcing that she was off to bed.

'Sweet dreams,' called Brodie with cheer.

Chastity pointed her nose towards the heavens as she left.

'You must forgive my daughter,' said Mr Klutter, 'she is young.'

'I'm twenty-six,' came the call from inside the wagon. 'And with good hearing.'

'My sisters were the same,' said Brodie, knowing that Chastity would be listening in. 'They had to be for our family to survive after my father's passing. I was the youngest and they brought me up. For that I thank them every day.'

Brodie was really stretching the truth here. His once a year, single Thanksgiving letter addressed to all four older siblings was testimony to his thrifty show of appreciation. However, like so many men, his silence masked much deeper, if unexpressed, feelings.

It is not known if Miss Chastity Klutter did have sweet dreams that evening but Brodie did. They were pleasant flights of fancy of sipping tea in a parlour. He, all spruced up, and she and her father seeking his superior knowledge on a wide range of subjects, which they keenly took in while nodding in appreciation.

Yes, he was showing the classic signs of being smitten. Something that can affect all men regardless of age. After all, he was 42 and she just 26; a gulf of sixteen whole years separated them, although the heart rarely concerns itself with such facts or figures.

The next morning Brodie felt an emptiness in the pit of his stomach when he came to say goodbye. Had they asked him to go with them, he would have had much difficulty in finding an excuse to say no. On no more than a whim, he very nearly offered. However, the foolishness of such a notion needed to be dismissed out of hand. Anyway, he had a plan and the thought of reversing it and going back to Death Valley to mine in an area that held little hope was enough to tip the scales away from such a flippant flight of fancy.

When he went to say his farewells, Chastity said, 'Does this belong to you?' She was holding up the small tuft of feathers from the Skidoo.'

He felt his top pocket. It was gone. 'It must have fallen out,' he said.

She looked at it closely. 'Pretty. A lucky charm?'

'Something like that,' he replied.

'Indian?'

'Timbisha Shoshone. Their home is Death Valley.'

'Very pretty. You should be more careful. I found it on the ground. Here, give me your hat and I'll secure it to the band.' When she handed his hat back and he put it on his head, she said, 'It looks good. It suits you.'

Brodie smiled self-consciously in response.

Mr Klutter put out his hand. The grip was firm and his smile genial. Brodie was about to tip his hat to Chastity when she stepped forward with her hand extended. He took it, but this time he didn't instantly let go. He held it for a second or two. Or was it even three or four? It was soft and warm, and he could smell her lavender scent. 'May you achieve all your dreams, Miss Klutter,' he said, not quiet knowing where the words had come from.

Chastity said in return, 'Thank you Mr Brodie, and may your dreams also be fulfilled.'

Brodie half-turned, but something inside told him not to leave with the regret of being so dismissive of this young woman's abilities and determination. 'Mining is a funny business,' he said, 'it's all about swinging a pick at just the right spot. And who is to say you won't find exactly where that is and strike a bonanza?'

And with that he turned, took up the lead on his mules and began to walk west. A trace of lavender lingered in the air and all the while he so desperately wanted to look back for one last glimpse of Miss Chastity Klutter.

SEVEN

CARNAGE
Tears of Sorrow

Each step now increased the distance from the person Brodie couldn't stop thinking about, and with each turn of the Klutters' wagon wheel the separation multiplied. Brodie was so completely preoccupied with his thoughts of Miss Klutter, how she looked, spoke and moved, that on three occasions he nearly tripped over, failing to see the most obvious of obstacles in his path.

His mules observed this distracted state of their master and instinctively knew that something was remiss. Not a word was spoken to them all day and Brodie seemed oblivious to all sorts of everyday occurrences. When unpacking the mules to make camp near an outcrop of rocks that hid their presence from the road, he didn't even hear the team of horses that passed by. Yet, they were less than two hundred paces away. Had Brodie been paying attention he would have been alerted by his mules lifting their heads as one, along with their upright ears that followed the sound of the four horsemen and their two spare horses carrying supplies. They were travelling in the direction of Death Valley and having made good time since leaving Cartago, would probably catch up to the Klutters by mid-afternoon the following day.

That evening the mules also observed that Brodie didn't eat a thing. He just drank coffee and gazed up at the stars that were brilliantly bright on that clear, cool night. However, when he started humming to himself the lament, *She Waits by the River for Me*, they wondered if he was going slightly loco.

Chastity Klutter had also lost her appetite as she looked up at those same stars. She kept recalling Brodie and their goodbye. He had apologised and wished her well, not just by his words but with his eyes. She had seen it. When he walked away with his mules, she had prayed that he would turn and give her one last wave so that she could do the same.

When her father had said, 'Time to go,' she just stood and watched, until he was out of sight.

Mr Klutter could see that his daughter was actually pining a little and it was a surprise. She'd had many admirers over the years. Good young men from good families and members of their church. Yet none had turned her head. Then Brodie appeared, said a few words of disparagement, apologized and left.

How odd, he thought, before saying with excitement, 'Today is a new day. Who knows what it will bring?'

'Is this a foolish dream, father?' queried Chastity. 'After all, I was the one who talked you into pursuing this venture.'

'No, you didn't. I am a willing participant in this enterprise, be it good, bad or indifferent. We have set our course so let's see where it takes us. Nothing ventured, nothing gained. And I am sure we will meet others like Mr Robert Brodie on the way.'

Chastity Klutter didn't think so. She had never met anyone like him before. There was something about Brodie that was different. Exactly what that was, she couldn't quite put her finger on, but she knew that they were intended to meet somewhere at some time for some good reason. Maybe it was destiny, maybe it was written in the stars.

The following day was much the same. The look upon Brodie's long face was that of a man trying to console himself with the false belief that time would quickly erase any memory of Miss Chastity Klutter. It was only due to a pungent smell in the morning air that Brodie was separated from his infatuated thoughts. He had missed seeing the smoke earlier. His eyes had been downcast. The stink came in wafts, between clean air, and had a sickly stench to it. Brodie knew immediately what it was. He'd smelt it during the war. It contained the sulphurous odour from burnt hair and the charcoal reek from burnt skin. The origin of the black smoke was not far off as

64

it drifted vertically in thin wisps. Brodie turned to the mules and simply said, 'This way,' while a dread swept over him.

He found the smouldering burnt-out wagon first. The oxen had both been shot and remained joined by their yoke, side-by-side, crumpled to the ground with the dirt soaked red around their noses. The wheels on one side of the wagon had fallen from the axles and caused what was left of the chassis to collapse to the ground, exposing the contents. Amongst the blackened belongings were two charred bodies. One an adult, the other an infant. A third body lay a little way off.

Brodie made his way to the corpse, still leading the mules. It was a man lying on his back with a wound to his forehead. The powder marks showed that he had been shot at close range. Were the perpetrators Indian, he wondered. He knew that it was not Timbisha Shoshone but could it be raiding Apache renegades this far west? If not, who would do such a savage thing to a lone settler family? They were of no threat and would have little of value to steal. Brodie continued to walk slowly around the scene, looking at the hoof prints. Amongst the scattered items was a cooking pan, a fork, two books lying face up and open, their pages turning in the light breeze, and a woman's night dress.

Brodie bit at his lip and he could feel the anger rising. He cursed and spat upon the ground. 'Whoever you are that did this wrong, may you rot in hell for it.'

As he went to pull the shovel from under the ropes of Corporal Jones' pack, Brodie caught sight of a fourth body. It was a woman some little distance off, lying face down, feet towards him, one shoe missing, the sole of her foot bleach white, and her dress hitched up a little. With his hand still on the shovel, he let his head drop onto his mule's neck as he took in three deep breaths. It had been twenty years since he'd seen such carnage, but that familiar feeling of futility came flooding back as if it were yesterday. 'Ah, geezes,' he said as he lifted his head, sucked in another deep breath and went to investigate.

The shot to the back was clear to see, a little to the right of middle. Brodie rolled her over gently and saw the face of an angel, eyes closed, appearing to be perfectly at peace. The skin was pale, yet the lips still retained a little colour, which surprised him. He put the back of his hand to her cheek, it was slightly warm. There was no blood to show a wound to the chest, therefore, the bullet had lodged within the body. He put his ear to her lips and while he had difficulty hearing for a breath, he could feel it ever so slightly. He lifted her up and carried her in his arms back to the mules and placed her in the shade of an overhanging rock. As he did, her eyes parted slightly, then widened with fear. Her mouth opened to let out a scream, but it turned into a cough and some specks of blood appeared on her bottom lip.

'It's alright.' said Brodie, 'you are safe now. I'm here to look after you.'

Her eyes continued to show alarm, so Brodie did what he had done with dying soldiers during the war. He held and patted her hand while reassuring her that she was now safe. 'My name is Robert Brodie. What's yours?'

With difficulty she said, 'Please don't hurt me.'

He continued to pat her hand, while shaking his head, 'I would never do that.'

She seemed to settle before giving another little cough and this time blood frothed from the corner of her mouth. 'Han,' she swallowed and tried again, 'Hannah.'

Brodie nodded. 'Hannah, were you attacked by Indians?'

She shook her head slightly and closed her eyes.

'Do you know who?'

Another difficult swallow before saying, 'Four.' Her eyes remained closed.

'Four men?'

A slight nod and cough.

Brodie took a water canteen from the pack, unscrewed the cap and put it to her lips. The water flooded over her chin as she tried to drink, so he filled the cap of the canteen and placed it to Hannah's mouth.

This time she failed to respond.

Brodie reached for her hand and slowly shifted his weight to take up a sitting position beside her, and once again he began to pat and gently caress the skin until she was cold. He was not a man given to sentiment. He believed that it had deserted him, bit by bit, during the war to leave him empty and numb. But now, inexplicably, his eyes filled with moisture and his tears splashed upon the apron bib of Hannah Olsen from Beaumont, the daughter of Joseph and wife Ada and big sister to baby Eden, who were on their way to Salt Lake City to settle. A gentle Mormon family who had been brutally murdered by four men. His weeping caused him no embarrassment. It was for the innocent now lost to the world forever.

Brodie dug four graves that early afternoon, one for each member of the family, but in the end only used three. Choosing to lay the small body of the infant with his mother. They had died together so he decided it was best that they stay together. Each body he wrapped in the remnants of the wagon's bonnet, cut into shape and lengths as required using the knife from his belt. He wrapped Hannah last and as he did, he saw the smudge of blood on the front of her dress between the legs. It looked like it had seeped through the fabric. He guessed as to its significance but couldn't bear to think about the cause as he stitched up the shroud to hide the damage done to her young body.

As gently as possible, he placed each into their grave and returned the earth upon them, leaving the fourth hole empty. He then fashioned a single cross with two spokes from a wagon wheel and laid it upon the father's grave. His wife and son on one side, his daughter on the other.

One of the books lying upon the ground was the family's book of prayer and inside were their names and dates of birth. Hannah was just sixteen and Eden four. His work now done, he stood before the family, took off his hat and, searching for something to say, could only think of the farewell, God speed, which seemed inappropriate. Lost for words and thinking from the top of his head, he said, 'May the Divine Wind carry you to heaven together,' before adding, 'Amen.'

All thoughts of Miss Chastity Klutter had been pushed from Brodie's mind by a deep feeling of despair. He had only briefly met one member of the Olsen family, but somehow he felt very close to all of them. He was now their chief mourner, their only mourner. On taking up the lead on Sergeant Smith to leave this pitiful place and continue on his journey, a breeze picked up and began to blow upon Brodie's face. The further he stepped out, the stronger it got until it started to pick up some dust, which blew into his eye, causing him to stop. When he did, so did the wind.

He stood, wiped the eye clear, looked around, expecting to see the wind and dust blowing away behind him, yet all seemed still. It was odd, but Brodie didn't think that it deserved any further thought until he stepped off again. And again, the breeze began to pick up and once again dust started coming his way. He turned his face to one side and stopped – and so did the wind.

Brodie wasn't unsettled by the event. He once again considered it odd and once again returned to his journey. And once again the breeze picked up and blew dust. But this time he was ready for it. He hoisted his bandana above his nose, gritted his teeth, pulled down on the brim of his hat and pushed on. And as he did the wind became stronger and colder until it was biting at his fingers and loosening the grip on his hat.

It flew off in a flurry to roll like the wheel of a cart for a good one hundred paces behind him.

He stopped to get his hat and the wind stopped.

'This is madness,' he told Smith, who like Jones had come to the same conclusion. Brodie turned the mules and as he walked back the breeze started up only this time it was light and warm. It only became stronger when he bent over to retrieve his hat, causing it to blow another ten paces further along. This pattern of follow, reach, follow, reach, happened three times. 'I give up,' he said looking to the sky. 'What the hell is going on?'

The reply he received was silence, but he knew something peculiar, beyond nature, was at play. Either that or he was going mad.

Sergeant Smith put his nose against Brodie's back and nudged. The response was one of annoyance. 'Are you in on this too?' He stood and looked at his hat while thinking, why am I being forced in this direction? I don't want to go back. I don't want to see Death Valley ever a–

And that's when he got it.

It was where Chastity Klutter and her father were heading. To the Skidoo. Were they now in danger from those who had attacked the Olsen family? Brodie stepped forward and reached for his hat, but hesitated. It didn't move. He snatched, gripped the crown, placed it upon his head and began to walk east, and as he did he felt the wind push against his back to help him along.

EIGHT

WHITE KNIGHT
A Message

Brodie was at full stride as frantic thoughts now swirled around his head of care and protection for Chastity and her father. These were somewhat perplexing notions for someone who had spent the best part of a lifetime only looking after themselves. Add to this the vicious reminder of the unfairness and fragility of life, when one so young and innocent as Hannah could be so cruelly and violently snatched away.

Brodie had once believed in the myth of invincibility – that fanciful belief gifted to all young men. Not anymore. After surviving three years of war and numerous mining accidents, including falling down shafts, almost being crushed by ore wagons, or being on the wrong side of a cave-in, he now knew better.

All life was fragile, including his. The only reason he wasn't dead was more often than not due to plain stupid luck, rather than good judgement. And as for being a protector of somebody else, what could he have possibly done for the Olsen family had he been there at the time of the confrontation? He was no hired gun, no pistolero or shootist. Sure, he'd been a soldier but that was twenty years ago, fighting in an army, never on his own, not like Sheriff Earp of Tombstone or Lincoln County's Sheriff Garrett. If he was going to defend the Klutters, the best way to do it, he concluded, was to avoid a fight with these four men at all costs. However, this internal dialogue led him to the terrible thought. What if Chastity and Frederick had already been attacked?

He didn't wish to contemplate such an idea, pushing it from his mind by walking faster, each step now coming with renewed urgency and a clear purpose. He must first find Chastity Klutter and her father, and then he must secure their safety. After that? Well, he wasn't too sure. He'd just have to figure that out along the way.

Brodie walked for the rest of the day and into the night following the road back the way he had come. The pace was fast and the strides long. By around midnight he was back to his previous night's camp. He stopped and watered the mules from his hat, but they took little and showed no signs of fatigue or soreness as he checked each leg. There was nothing to stop him from pressing on relentlessly into the morning light and beyond. And that's what he did, non-stop, in a continuous and constant forced march. One man and two mules on a frantic dash of mercy.

It was just before midday when he found what was left of the Klutters' wagon. It too had been partially burnt and the goods scattered. Frederick Klutter had come to rest on his side, shot through the neck, and it looked to Brodie like he had fallen from the wagon seat to the ground where he now lay. The oxen were also dead, both being shot between the eyes.

With desperation he searched for Chastity and could find no sign of her anywhere. He climbed atop of some rocks to get a better view, then commenced to walk in circles around the wagon, each time a little wider in a frantic effort to find some sign of where she may have gone. After a fruitless hour of searching, he had no choice but to come to the conclusion that she had been taken. The thought of what would now befall her started to make him tremble with the fear of the consequences. He would have to go after these four men as best he could, following the tracks left by their horses.

He was torn as to what to do with Frederick Klutter's body. He needed to get going if he was to have any chance of catching up, but to leave the body crumpled upon the ground for the flies seemed wrong. There was no choice, he concluded; he had to go, and now.

And that's when the smell of lavender wafted in on a light breeze.

It was so strong, as if Chastity had just passed by, and it made Brodie stop and sniff the air as if he was some kind of hound. He stepped forward and began to walk up a rise towards a large rocky outcrop some three hundred yards away, and all the time the smell of lavender remained fresh upon the air. Once at the outcrop he stopped, yet the fragrance continued to swirl on the breeze. It was bizarre and disturbing, like being enticed, but to what? He could see no place where she could be. He turned around and as he began to walk back down the slope a cold breeze blew directly into his face. He stopped, hung his head. 'OK,' he said. 'I get it,' and turned back around. But what to do? A solid wall of rock stood before him as the smell of lavender returned. Confused, Brodie started to weave his way between the smaller rocks until he was within an arm's reach of the sheer face while trying to determine where the aroma was strongest.

To the right, down low at the base of the wall, were a series of small, narrow gaps. Brodie went to each one, sniffing. At the last, when he lay down to look in, a soothing breeze blew upon his face. 'Chastity?' he called self-consciously, 'are you in there?'

And from the dark came the reply, 'Brodie? Is that you?'

'Yes, yes, it is. It's Brodie, are you OK in there?'

He could hear the noise of someone squirming their way towards him. He waited and heard what sounded like the echo of 'darn', before a hand popped out of the dark.

'You're going to have to pull me out.' Her second hand appeared.

'How did you get in there? We'll never get you out.'

'Yes, you will, just pull.'

Brodie grabbed both wrists and Chastity wrapped her fingers around his wrists. Taking up a sitting position with his legs apart and feet against the rock wall, he slowly lent back and began to pull as gently as he could. Slowly, Chastity Klutter began to emerge, a bit like a snake as she kept her tight grip on Brodie's wrists and wiggled her hips to assist in the extrication. When her legs were finally free, she pulled herself up onto her knees to lurch into Brodie's arms and give him a tight hug.

Brodie slowly folded his arms around her and patted her back.

'I knew you'd come for me. I knew it. I prayed, and I knew that my prayers would be answered. You are my saviour, my white knight, Robert Brodie, and I say praise the Lord.'

Brodie felt a complete sense of relief wash over his body from head to foot. His concerns and worries were swept away. Chastity Klutter had been delivered into his arms. Carefully, he squeezed, and she responded with vigour.

'You smell so good,' she said.

'And you. I like lavender.'

'Lavender? I haven't been wearing lavender for days.' She sniffed at her dress by pulling the top of her apron out a little. 'Can't smell it. But you, what is that?'

'Almonds, I've been told. Roasted almonds but I'm unable to pick it up.'

'Is too, fancy that. Like almonds in a fruit cake. Where does it come from?'

'I have no idea, it just turned up.'

'And you say you can smell lavender on me.'

Brodie sniffed. 'I can. Not as strong as before, but it's there.'

'How odd,' said Chastity Klutter and gave Brodie another hug before kneeling up in front of him. 'I see you still have your Indian charm where I placed it.'

Brodie took his hat from his head to check. 'Yes, it is still there, right where you placed it.' He glanced to one side before saying, 'Your father is down by the wagon. He's passed.'

'I know,' said Chastity. 'Best I go to him.'

'Are you sure?'

Chastity pressed her lips tight and nodded her head.

'Frederick has been lying in the sun. The heat has had its effect. Best to remember him as he was.'

'I also prayed for my father's soul, but I still need to say my goodbyes.'

'Do that when we bury him. Let me prepare the body as best I can.'

Chasity wiped her eyes with a cuff and nodded.

'OK?' he asked, seeking confirmation.

She nodded her head again.

'You need some water and I need to know what happened.'

Brodie escorted her back down to the mules, choosing a path that took her away from the body of her father.

She drank long and hard from the canteen while telling of four men who overtook them and rode on by. Her father had given them a wave but received none in return. Several hours later they caught sight of the men waiting up ahead on the side of the road.

Mr Klutter said to his daughter, 'Fetch my shotgun from the back.'

She slipped off the seat into the wagon and was just reaching for the gun when her father was shot.

He fell to the ground, clutching his neck, but was still able to call to Chastity, 'Hide girl.'

But where? They had seen her and if she stayed in the wagon, she'd be trapped. In desperation, she leapt from the back and ran.

She was a good fifty paces away before they saw that she was trying to escape.

One called out, 'It doesn't matter, sweetheart, we'll get you. You've got nowhere to run to out here.'

One of the other men called, 'I'll get her, Jake.'

The reply from Jake was, 'No, you sort through their belongings, I'll go get her.'

Chastity was up to the rocks when she turned to see the man called Jake walking up the slope behind her in no hurry and pulling the belt from his pants.

She had inadvertently run into a dead end. Her only thought was to skirt around the rock face. In fear for her life and her virtue, she saw the small entrance. It was her only chance. With difficulty and determination, she squirmed her way in, just being able to wriggle down the narrow tunnel, which mercifully opened into a larger chamber where she could turn around, sit with knees under her chin, and stare back at the tiny entrance.

She could hear Jake outside cussing and somewhat bewildered as to where she had gone. He was then joined by the others and one of the men actually got down and looked into her hiding place, saying, 'Do you think she coulda crawled in here?'

Jake replied sharply, 'You couldn't get a jackrabbit in there. She must have hid behind the rocks and doubled back around to the other side. We'll look for her when we go out that way.'

As darkness fell, she had no way of knowing if her attackers had gone or were waiting for her. Alone and fearful of crawling out of her little grotto, she began to pray to the Lord for a saviour. 'And that saviour was you, Robert Brodie, and in my heart of hearts I knew you would come.'

Brodie listened to the story with a degree of astonishment but also pride. Pride in the faith she had in him and astonishment at her ingenuity to survive by crawling through an opening the size of a breadbox.

'But why did you know?' he asked. 'Was it because I was the closest traveller?'

'It came in a beautiful dream,' said Chastity. 'I just knew in my heart you wouldn't forget me. Was I right?'

Brodie nodded in agreement. 'Yes, you were. You have preoccupied my thoughts since we parted.'

'Mine too.'

Brodie decided not to tell her about the wind that guided him back to her. It would have sounded all too silly for words, but he did tell of what had happened to the Olson family, although he did his best not to alarm and upset her. What he did confirm, however, was that the same four men had been involved in both unprovoked attacks. He then took her hand in his hands, as he had done with Hannah, and said that he would protect her. He also told her to rest on his bedroll while he took the shovel and went off to dig a grave for her father.

Brodie dug the hole deep and made sure that its length and width would fully accommodate Frederick's body. He'd seen soldiers returned to the earth scrunched up in their graves and he always thought that it stole the last of their dignity. He then set about the arrangements as he had done for the Olsen family. He laid Mr Klutter upon a canvas sheet cut from the bonnet of the wagon. He pulled the shroud tight and stitched it up, starting at the feet. He left it open from the waist to show the hands, which he crossed upon the chest. The hood of the pall he tucked around the face to partially hide the bloating, and he rubbed a little dust on the cheeks to hide the darkening of the skin. A smell was present, but this he disguised by taking some orange peel that he found near the wagon and placing it under the collar.

He returned to Chastity to find that she was in a dead sleep. He left her that way until the sun was low on the horizon and gently woke her.

She shot bolt upright in fright.

'It's alright,' he said quietly. 'I'm here, you're safe. It's time to say goodbye to your father.

Chastity quickly composed herself. 'Yes,' she said, 'the funeral arrangements need to go ahead.'

Silently, he escorted her across to the body. She knelt down and touched the face before leaning in to kiss the forehead. Brodie put his hand under her arm and helped lift and steady her to her feet. She was now quietly weeping, making a soft murmuring sound. He went to escort her back to their little camp, when she asked, 'My father's gold pocket watch. He always kept it with him. Do you have it?'

'No,' said Brodie. 'I checked all the pockets and they were turned inside out and the fob pocket on the vest was ripped open.'

Chastity just nodded as if in silent acceptance that it was expected to be so.

Brodie took her back to where he had laid out a dish and canteen nearby. 'You wash up. When ready, I'll come and get you and we'll conduct a service.'

Chastity Klutter seemed to deflate to the ground as she sat back down upon his bedroll.

Brodie returned to the body, stitched up the shroud, placed the body into the hole and quickly and quietly buried Frederick. He then smudged the marks with his boot, where the body had been dragged across the ground to the grave.

He returned to Chastity, took her hand and led her back as the light was fading fast. At this particular point, he wasn't exactly sure what should occur next, other than a prayer of remembrance. This is where the 26-year-old Miss Klutter surprised him. Somehow, she had been able to recompose herself and take back control. She walked past the grave and went to the back of the half-burnt wagon and rummaged around in the scattered items. In the drawer of her small sewing machine, she took out a soft covered Bible with onionskin-thin pages and returned.

Brodie glanced at the book. It seemed so small and personal, and in his mind it reflected the circumstances of a family that consisted of just two people, her and her father.

At the end of the grave standing side-by-side, Chastity asked Brodie, 'Would you be so kind as to commence the service for me Robert and commit my father to his grave.'

How? he thought. He'd already shrouded and buried the poor man. What else could he do? Without thinking, he came to attention, as he had done at so many military funerals, and said, 'We stand here before you, Oh Lord, to commit Frederick Klutter—'

82

Chastity bumped his shoulder slightly and said in a low voice, 'Frederick Barnaby Klutter.'

Brodie corrected himself with a lifted voice as if announcing to a full guard of honour, 'We commit Frederick Barnaby Klutter to the earth and his soul into your hands.' At this point he ran out of words and was now in a dilemma as what to say next.

Thankfully, Chastity stepped in by saying, 'We release him into your care oh Lord, knowing that you will welcome him into the Kingdom of Heaven.' She then commenced to sing *Abide with Me*, which thankfully was the only hymn that Robert Brodie knew and was able to mumble along to, while Chastity sang in a beautifully sweet voice.

When finished, she announced, 'I will now read a passage from the Bible.' On opening the book, she went to read, just as a soft wind blew to flutter the thin pages. 'Darn,' she said, 'Lost my place.' She scrambled back the pages and went to read. Once again, the wind blew the pages over. She repeated her actions and the wind followed.

Brodie knew this game. It was familiar. It was no good fighting the wind. 'We are losing the light. I suggest that you just read where the wind opens the page,' adding, 'It's probably providence.'

Chastity looked closely in the poor light as she began to read. 'This is from John 14. Do not let your hearts be troubled. You believe in God. My Father's house has many rooms…'

It was an appropriate verse and Brodie nodded in agreement as Chastity read it in a clear and confident manner.

When she had finished, the wind blew the pages again to a new spot in the Bible and Chastity said, 'Providence again, I'll read this too. It is from Leviticus 24, 18. 'Whoever kills an animal must make restitution. Anyone who injures their neighbour is to be injured in the same manner: fracture for fracture, eye for eye, tooth for tooth. As he has done, so shall it be done to him.'

Silence followed before Chastity said, 'Robert, the Lord has sent us a message. It *is* providence. We must now do what has been spoken.'

NINE

THE SEARCH

The Lord's Work

Exactly what that message was from the Lord was lost on Brodie, but he could kind of guess where it was leading. Reluctantly, he said, 'What message is that?'

'I prayed that you would return and save me. The devil may have cast his evil, but it was the Lord who sent his best helper.'

Brodie said, 'I wish he had sent me earlier to save the Olsens.'

'You can now, Robert.'

'How?' he asked more than a little puzzled.

'By doing the Lord's work and removing the evil that befell the Olsen family and my father. The Lord has spoken.'

Brodie wasn't sure that's what was being said at all by the Good Lord. He'd seen some pages being shuffled by the wind and foolishly hinted that maybe it was fate at work. Had he known that this was going to fire up Chastity on a crusade of Christian retribution, he would have been more prudent with his comments. The last thing he wanted to do was dole out justice with a young woman who was lucky to escape with her own life and honour intact. Sure, he wanted retribution for what had been done by this gang of four, led by this Jake character, and yes, he would bear witness in a court of law to what he had heard from Hannah and seen with his own eyes. But while he still held grief and anger in his heart, he really didn't want to be either a crusader or a white knight. He had come back for Chastity Klutter, albeit after a push and shove by the Divine Wind or whatever it was at work, but it had been to find and protect her, not to deliver vengeance.

This dilemma made Brodie feel very uncomfortable. Was he being weak? Was he showing a lack of courage when he should be showing strength? Was he looking for a way out?

Chastity remained adamant. 'Those four men are evil, and they need to be dealt with.'

That, Brodie couldn't dispute, but the question was, 'How?' he asked.

'We smite them.'

'Smite?' repeated Brodie.

'Yes,' came the precise and unequivocal reply.

'You mean kill?' Brodie wanted to get this straight.

'Yes,' said Chastity emphatically. 'In the name of the Lord.'

'It should be in the name of the law.'

'The Lord *is* the law, and the law is about balancing the scales of justice.'

'Be it about balancing the scales of justice or not, the Lord won't be doing the killing.'

'No,' said Chastity, 'we will have to do that for him.'

Brodie mulled over the 'we' and asked with a little more than a touch of mockery, 'I'm guessing, you haven't done much killing in your life up till now?'

'No, never, but I witnessed my father's murder, so I am now ready and happy to pull the trigger. Have *you* done much killing?' she asked.

'During the war, not after, I've had no need.'

'But you have experience. It's not hard to do then?'

'No,' said Brodie. 'The act of killing isn't difficult to do with a gun. It's the residue it leaves behind that is difficult to erase.'

'How so?' asked Chastity, and she was genuine in her keen enquiry.

'It leaves you with recollections that are kind of unsettling and hard to get out of your head.'

'Surely not against murderers and thieves when done in the name of the Lord?'

Brodie did feel anger at what had been done by these men, but he also knew how emotions could change over time. 'A life is a life, regardless,' he said. 'Somehow, the moral judgement doesn't seem to count that much as the years pass. Hating the enemy gets lost after the first battle,' said Brodie reflectively.

'But these are not soldiers fighting for a just cause,' said Chastity.

'That is true,' said Brodie, realizing that he needed to take the lead and commit as Chastity was not going to let this go. 'If there is any killing to be done, I'll do it. I don't want you to have blood on your hands.'

'We will do it together,' confirmed Chastity with some enthusiasm.

Brodie needed to give some due warning into what was actually involved and provide perspective. He knew the odds were poor. 'It will be two against four.'

'The Lord will be on our side.'

'Let's just put the Lord to one side for the moment. If I was to be killed, for any reason, it would put you back in the same situation you were in when your father was killed. Isn't that of concern?'

'You are more than a match for those murderous criminals and when we recover my father's gold pocket watch, I want you to have it.'

The only saving grace, as Brodie could now see it, was that it would be near impossible to track down four men travelling at speed on horseback. Walking the mules, no matter how brisk, would not be enough. Maybe, just a show of effort would appease Chastity. 'I don't need a pocket watch, thank you. I have a good sense of time and that's all I need. If we do recover the timepiece, it should stay in your hands as a personal memento of your father.' Brodie now used this moment to propose a compromise by imposing a limit upon this undertaking. 'I have enough provisions for us to spend seven days searching. If we use all that time, it could mean two weeks before we are standing back here where we started. After that it could take up to three to four weeks to get you back home, depending. Feeding two mouths, we will be chewing on the corners of the canvas covers by the time we get anywhere near the Cajon Pass. Besides, if we haven't found them in seven days, they'll be well across the border and into Nevada or Arizona or wherever they are heading. So, seven days, no more. Do you understand?'

'Oh, I'm sure that we'll have them by then.'

'Don't be so sure. They are on horseback while we are on foot.'

'Yes, but the Lord will slow them down so that we may catch up.'

Brodie didn't comment other than to say that Chastity should collect any small personal belongings required for the journey ahead.

She held up the small Bible. 'This is all I need now.'

'What's the piece of paper sticking out of the back?' asked Brodie.

'It's the registered mining claim. Would you like to see it?'

Brodie shook his head. 'Not now, maybe later.'

When repacking the two mules, Chastity asked, 'Do your donkeys have names?'

Brodie bristled a little. 'They are mules and yes they have names. This one is Sergeant Smith and this one is Corporal Jones.'

'Smith and Jones?' Chastity pulled a little face of disparagement and it was noticed.

'I didn't name them that,' says Brodie. 'That's just how they came to me.'

'Bit common. Couldn't you have renamed them?'

'I was working a twenty-mule team with three other muleskinners who each worked a team of twenty. There was also the stock we ran in reserve to replace any of the lame or injured. A lot of mules meant names were in short supply. Besides, I didn't want to confuse them. Better to just promote them instead.'

'Promote them how?'

'Smithy was a corporal. I made him a sergeant. And Jones here was a private. He's now a corporal.'

'When did you do that?'

'When I purchased them from Harmony.'

'You own them outright?'

'Own?' Brodie shrugged. 'We work more as a team. Equal like.'

Chastity wasn't convinced about all this team parity talk. 'I've heard mules need a firm hand on account that they are bad tempered to the point of being mean and ornery.'

'That's donkeys. Mules are different. Treat them well and they will return the compliment. They just don't like being taken for granted.'

'That makes sense. I never liked being taken for granted either. It takes nothing to tell someone that their efforts are appreciated. Mind you, it should never be laid on too thick or it just becomes cheap words. A simple thank you will often suffice.'

The two mules nodded their heads.

'Seems they agree with you,' said Brodie.

'They are smart aren't they,' said Chastity.

'Sometimes too smart by half,' said Brodie under his breath.

'What about being stubborn?'

'I've met more stubborn people than mules, and I've known a lot of mules.'

'Well I do know one thing,' relented Chastity, 'without Sergeant Smith and Corporal Jones, we would never be able to carry all the supplies necessary to survive out here.'

'Ain't that the truth,' said Brodie. 'Without these boys we would be in deep trouble.'

TEN

SEVEN DAYS

Texans

The tracks of the horses were not difficult to follow as there was nothing to remove their imprints from the landscape. Some impressions, like wagon wheels, had been known to remain unspoilt on the desert floor for years. Once or twice a decade, the heavens would open in a thunderous downpour as if in excuse for their prolonged lethargy. Even then, it was usually contained and confined. Rain could be observed sweeping down from dark clouds at one end of the valley by someone further along who was being burnt up by the sun.

They followed the hoof prints towards Panamint Springs, where the tracks of the six horses only ventured off the road to make camp. The real difficulty facing Brodie was in telling exactly how much time had passed since the tracks had been laid. The size of one camp fire, made from dried mesquite, indicated that they had stayed for a while, but he knew they were at least two days ahead.

On the third day, the road passed over a wide shallow gully carved from the earth thousands of years before. Here, the tracks turned off towards the Panamint Range that forms the western wall of Death Valley. Brodie didn't know exactly where the four were heading. He thought maybe it was the silver mines of Panamint City, or did they know of some new way into Nevada or more south to Arizona. The known ways were via Stovepipe Wells or the Skidoo Pass, finding a fresh trail across the Panamint Range would be difficult if not downright dangerous. Many who had gone in there to search for the fabled Gunsight Lode had just disappeared, never to be seen or heard of again.

The only thing Brodie did know for sure was that once they entered the range, the chances of closing in and catching up would be gone. Brodie mentioned none of this to Chastity, who kept up with his fast pace without a word of complaint. With each step he did hope that maybe, somehow, she would come to realize the hopelessness of chasing horses on foot, even if those they were pursuing were travelling easy and making camp early. The gap they had to make up and the time available was just too great. Yet, Chastity showed no sign of faltering. She was going to stay the course for the full seven days; that was evident. However, in Brodie's mind, when that deadline did come there would be no further concessions, they would have to turn around. He would take her back to San Bernardino to her church. After that, well who knew? Although he did hold hopes for a future. The ties that bind were now being pulled tight.

On the fifth day, the tracks seemed to meander away from the foothills and on the sixth they led directly into a series of jagged ravines carved out of the landscape and baked solid. Some of the chasms were narrow while others opened up into shallow gullies before turning into tall mini canyons with steep sides twice the height of the average man. Brodie had no idea why anyone would want to venture here as it soon became apparent that they were in a maze. He now became concerned that he and Chastity could easily get lost in this tangle of geography.

By mid-afternoon on the seventh day, Brodie stopped and dug for water, which he found with relative ease.

'How did you do that?' asked Chastity.

'There's water under the ground most of the time. Sometimes you have to dig deep but below these old riverbeds it is still there, somewhere.'

Chastity took a long drink from the canteen and asked, 'Are you worried we could get lost in here? I am.'

Brodie seized on the opportunity to broach their return. 'And me. If we go much further, getting out of here could be a bit of a problem.'

'Really, I just took for granted that you knew.'

'No, I didn't even know this place existed.'

'So why are these Texans in here?'

'Texans? What makes you think they are from Texas?'

'I've been told that Texas is full of heathens, outlaws, sinners and drunkards, which fits the bill quite nicely for these four.'

Brodie felt obliged to defend his adopted state. 'My mother came from Texas before she moved on out to California with her family.'

'One of the smart ones that got away, then?' said Chastity without missing a beat. 'But you're not from Texas, are you?'

'No, I'm Californian born and bred, but I served Texas during the war.'

'You're a Confederate?'

'I'm not anything now, other than a muleskinner.'

'You are way more than that Robert Brodie. You are my saviour. If not for you, I'd be wandering around in circles trying to find my way back to civilization...' She looked at the hole where the mules were drinking, '...with no water and little hope, but you came along, sent by the Lord to save me.'

'But I'm not doing that out here, am I? Do you think it's high time that I start doing it now, and return you to your family in San Bernardino?'

'I don't have a family, other than the church, so there's no hurry there. But I have been expecting you to say that it was time to go back, being the seventh day and all.'

'I think time has run out,' reinforced Brodie.

Chastity looked around and up to the sky as the mules continued to drink. 'Yes, I guess so. We've come a long way and we have a long way to go back.' She nodded her head as if to confirm the decision to herself.

Brodie put his hand on Chastity's shoulder. 'We gave it a good try. We may as well turn around and move back down this ravine till nightfall, camp up and try to get out of this place by tomorrow.'

Brodie was checking the cinches on the mules as they prepared to leave, when a foul smell came wafting into the ravine.

'Oh, that's terrible,' said Chastity pulling a face and holding her nose. 'Smells like something is dead.'

Brodie put a finger to his lips for her to be silent. He knew exactly what that smell was. Someone close by, very close by, was defecating. He crawled up the steep side wall and peeked over the edge. Less than twenty paces away was a solidly built man with his pants down around his ankles.

ELEVEN

LET US PRAY

Ambush

Chastity crawled up next to Brodie and took a peek, gripping his arm and whispering into his ear. 'That's one, that's one of them. You have to shoot him.'

Brodie whispered back, 'If I shoot him, he'll alert the others.' Slowly, he pulled his Colt from the holster and turned it around in his hand, gripping the chamber.

'What are you going to do?'

'I'll have to knock him out,' whispered Brodie. 'We can drag him back here, tie and gag him. When the others come looking, we'll take each out with the rifle. If we get just one more the odds are even. Two against two.'

Just as Brodie slid over the top of the ravine to commence his approach, his quarry started to stand up.

Chastity, who had also crawled part way over the edge, felt a smooth grey rock the size of a fist beneath her hand. She grasped it and without thought jumped to her feet and let fly.

The missile sliced through the air fast and level, and to Brodie's astonishment struck its target on the left temple and knocked him to the ground unconscious.

'Come on,' called Chastity quietly, 'we've got him.'

The man lay on his back with his pants still around his ankles. Brodie holstered his pistol and, taking his belt from his waist, slipped off the knife still in its scabbard, turned their captive on his side and bound his hands behind his back. Just as he was rolled back, a groan signified that he was regaining consciousness. Brodie put his hand over the man's mouth and said to Chastity, 'Use my knife to cut the tail off his shirt, and we'll stuff it in his mouth.'

Chastity worked quickly, the sharp blade cleanly slicing the fabric across the lower front portion of the shirt, exposing dark hair upon the stomach. She handed the shirt tail to Brodie.

As he was stuffing it into the mouth, the man opened his eyes and, on seeing Chastity with the knife in her hand, became alarmed and started to kick, but with his pants still below his knees he was unable to make any contact.

Chastity glared at him for a moment, reached down to the genitals, grasped his penis in her left hand, pulled it upright and, with one quick slice of the knife, cut it off.

The terrified look in the man's eyes caused Brodie to glance down as to the reason why. He saw what Chastity had done and grimaced instinctively.

'He won't be using that anymore,' pronounced Chastity and placed the severed member on the man's chest, just below his chin.

'What have you done?' said Brodie in sheer bewilderment.

'This is the Lord's business. We are but his servants. Let us pray.'

The man slumped back into unconsciousness again as the blood now pumped freely from the wound between his legs.

Brodie shook his head. 'Believe me, Chastity, this is no time to pray. Let's get back to the ravine and wait in ambush for the others to come.' As he turned to go, he remembered his belt. 'Belt,' he called and rolled the body on its side, then quickly yanked at the buckle.

They had just made it into the gully when they heard the call, 'Chad, come on Chad, we've got to get out of this goddamn place. Will you hurry up?'

'Rifle,' said Brodie in an agitated whisper. 'I need my rifle. Keep watch, but don't be seen. And don't throw any more rocks.' He slid down the bank and raced across to the mules, pulled the Winchester from the rifle scabbard and returned to Chastity.

'Too late', she said. 'He came out, saw what had happened and raced back to disappear.'

'That quick?' questioned Brodie.

'That quick,' confirmed Chastity. 'He took off like a startled deer when he saw what had happened.'

'I bet he did,' was Brodie's response.

'Now what?' she asked.

'Now what, indeed. They will certainly be confused as to what they are up against, so we should take advantage of that situation.

'How?'

'That, I don't know. Never been put in a position quite like this before.'

'What would you have done in the Army of the South?'

'Storm their position straight away.'

'Should we do that now?' Chastity asked.

'Not unless we want to die. It only works with superior forces, and even then you should expect about a third in casualties.'

Chastity thought for a moment or two then said, 'One third of two aren't very good odds, so what else can we do?'

'First, we need to find them before they find us. Exactly where did he go?'

'Just to the front of us, maybe to the right a little, not more than fifty paces away.'

'That close?' Brodie hadn't realised just how close they had been to the men that they had spent the last seven days searching for.

DIVINE WIND

'What is the second thing we need to do?'

'Try to pick them off one at a time, but quietly, until we have one left. Then we can make as much noise as we like.'

'Do we use the knife?' Chastity held up Brodie's knife, which she had retained.

'Or maybe a rock to the head,' he quipped. 'Where did you learn to throw like that?'

'I used to work the knock 'em down stall at our church fair each year. Been doing it since I was twelve. I could always pitch a ball better than the boys. Straighter, harder and faster.'

'I noticed.'

'Thank you for noticing,' said Chastity in an almost chatty way.

'I also noticed your knife-cutting skills.' Brodie gave a little cough. 'Where did they come from?'

'Oh, that was just impulse. The only time I've ever used a knife as sharp as this is in the cook-house, but right at that moment it was as if the Lord was saying, time for an eye for an eye, a tooth for a tooth, a—'

Brodie cut Chastity short. 'Yeah, right, got it.'

'Maybe, they'll think they are up against a pack of savage Indians.' said Chastity.

'That would help to explain the...' Brodie paused, he couldn't find an appropriate word so settled on 'scalping', which was at least partially accurate.

'If they do, are they likely to run away and try to escape?'

'It would certainly cross my mind to do so,' said Brodie. 'Unless they have become lost in this maze and can't find their way out. If they have been wandering around in circles, it would explain how we managed to catch up to them.' Brodie decided that it was a good time to ask, 'Do you think maybe we should just go? We got one and I'm sure we've scared the hell out of the other three.'

Chastity half smiled. 'If it had been Jake I'd say yes. But I know what he was really after and had he got it I wouldn't have wanted to live. Besides, we are on to 'em and they are close by. We just need to finish the Lord's business.'

'Are you sure this is the Lord's business?' asked Brodie.

'Sure, I'm sure. The souls of that poor family and my father, and others, of that I have no doubt, can only rest when the balance sheet is set right.'

Brodie didn't know how to respond to such a righteous statement, so he just repeated her last word, 'Right.' But it wasn't said with any sense of agreement.

Chastity took a peek over the edge of their ravine. 'Will they come and get him?' She tilted her head towards the body lying some twenty paces away.

Brodie shrugged. 'I don't know. Maybe, if they want his gun they will, but then again, they have plenty of guns.'

'They have my father's shotgun,' said Chastity wistfully. 'It's a fine gun. Embossed with a little jumping deer. My pa taught me how to shoot ducks in flight with it.'

'Did you get to bag any?'

'I sure did. We were eating so many ducks there for a while, we just got plain sick of 'em. Boy-o-boy would I love a slice of duck pie now. I'm over pork and beans, at least for now.' Without taking a breath, Chastity asked, 'So, do we go and get these Texans?'

Brodie had to turn his head to hide his wry smile. This woman who had taken his heart could be so surprisingly amusing at times without even knowing it. She was indeed an intriguing mix of contradictions with most being favourable, some extraordinary and one or two quite alarming. And strangely, at her core was her faith that allowed her to expound on the importance of virtue, righteousness and vengeance all at once. She was also able to contain and conceal both the horror and the sorrow she must be feeling for the murder and loss of her father. She was always optimistic and could think on her feet, as shown by the ingenuity in finding a place to hide at the base of a rocky wall. Her courage was undisputed, as demonstrated by her rock-throwing ability and willingness to take action. She was also tough. Her grit and determination had been displayed daily by tramping besides him at a fast pace, without a grumble, for mile after mile, day after day.

And then there was the curiosity she evoked in Brodie.

This young woman, with the trim figure and an impertinence to her manner, had a confidence that seemed totally uninhibited. It was Brodie who had to turn away when she washed, rubbing a moist cloth over her bare shoulders and even under her extended arms, and all without the slightest of concerns. She would also announce to him when she was off to the 'ladies' room' while calling for him not to leave without her, as she disappeared behind a rock. Then, of course, there were the unpredictable aspects of this practical girl, like cutting off–

He stopped his thoughts from going any further and said, 'Let's just wait a little while to see if these Texans do show up.'

They waited quietly in ambush, Brodie peeking over the edge with Chastity tucked up next to him also on sentry. The body lay on its back with unblinking eyes looking towards the heavens, acting as the bait that they hoped would draw out the other 'Texans'.

But nobody came.

Chastity was getting a little bored with this game of patience and said to Brodie, 'Guess his soul is now in hell.'

Brodie didn't want to get into a debate on the whereabouts of souls, be they good or bad, and he knew that to get distracted, when in ambush, was usually the time when the enemy appeared. 'Guess,' was all he said.

'Do you think they are coming at all?' asked Chastity.

'Don't know.'

'Been a while.'

Brodie agreed, 'A while. Could be longer.'

'How much longer?'

'Don't know.'

'So how long are we going to wait?'

'Till nightfall, when we can't see.'

'That long?'

'Be an hour, not much more.'

Chastity took another peek over the edge of the gully and tilted her head towards the body. 'I don't think they are going to come for him.'

Brodie shook his head. 'It doesn't look like it.'

'I thought soldiers recovered their dead.'

'They do, but these are not soldiers. They have no honour or commitment to a higher cause, just themselves.'

'You're right, these are Tex—' she checked herself. 'These are murderous heathens without a scruple of honour.'

TWELVE

VOICES IN THE NIGHT

Lost Time

As the evening light began to fade, they quietly slid back down from the top of the ravine and joined the mules.

'Just sit tight for a minute,' Brodie told Chastity. 'I'm going to take a quick look forward. I want to make sure it is clear while we still have a little light.

Chastity's eyes showed a little apprehension at being left alone.

'A few minutes, no more,' said Brodie to appease any concern. 'It's for our safety.'

Reluctantly, Chastity said, 'OK, a minute.'

'Or two,' he added, and with the Winchester in his hand, he slowly walked up the ravine and into the shadows.

The light had gone by the time Brodie returned to find Chastity on edge. 'I was worried,' she said, 'you seemed to be gone for a good while.'

'Just a few minutes. Maybe, ten.'

'Seemed longer.'

'The night can do that.' He took her hand. 'It looks clear from the little I could see. We'll stay here the night.' Brodie stepped across to the mules and began to strip down their packs.

'Will they come looking for us?' asked Chastity.

'Doubt it,' said Brodie, as he passed her a strip of dried salted beef. 'Too dark, but we still need to remain armed and alert. Best you take your bonnet off, so your ears aren't covered. We'll need to listen for any sounds, no matter how small. You can tuck yourself in against the wall here. I'll dig it out a little first to help hide any silhouette. I'll be over against the other wall and do the same.'

Chastity put the beef to her lips but didn't bite. 'I would much prefer that we stay together, close. If I'm on my own and they sneak up and murder me, I'd rather that it be done in your company than on my own.'

Brodie knew that they should have two sentries posted in two separate locations to guard the most likely approaches – the direction they were heading, and the one from where they had come. Yet, without a word, he relented. The thought of having Chastity close to him was too enticing. He liked it when she was close, very close. She smelt of lavender and always seemed so neat and clean, even under these harsh conditions. It was as if she was some sort of exotic creature from one of those Greek myths. Someone set apart from mere mortals like himself.

After digging out a small bay in the side of the ravine, they settled in. It was a snug fit, but neither complained. After an hour, he felt Chastity's head fall heavy upon his shoulder. He chose not to wake her. The sensation of having a sleeping woman resting against him was just too captivating.

Brodie was fighting to stay vigilant when Corporal Jones alerted him. He was lightly pawing the ground with an outstretched hoof. Chastity's head remained undisturbed on Brodie's shoulder; her hair soft upon the side of his whiskered face. She was in a deep sleep.

He listened as Jones scuffed again, as if to say, it's still there. Brodie turned his head, slightly, straining to hear. Was it an animal? But what animal? They had seen no sign of any wildlife, not even birds. Then the unmistakable sound of voices. Not loud, not that could be understood, but voices nevertheless, muffled, in conversation, not wishing to announce their presence.

Chastity stirred and Brodie quickly slid his hand across her mouth to suppress any sound of surprise. 'We have visitors,' he said quietly.

Chastity's head jerked upright.

'Easy, they don't know we are here.' He released his grip and felt her breath expel warm upon his palm. Gently, he pulled his Colt from the holster and placed it in her lap. 'Stay here,' he said, as he lifted the Winchester from the ground where he had placed it by his side. 'I'll check it out.'

Chastity tilted her head to hear the muffled voices. 'Why don't we just shoot them from here?' she whispered.

'Have to see what we are firing at to hit a target, and we need to make sure we're not shooting at innocent travellers,' said Brodie quietly, before adding, 'although I doubt that somehow. Not in this maze and moving at night.'

'I want to go with you.'

'No, you stay right here and keep my pistol at the ready, but don't shoot until you can clearly identify a target. I don't want you shooting me.' Brodie patted her knee to provide comfort. 'Whoever it is, they don't know we are here or that we are after them. We have the upper hand.'

As he edged forward in a crouch with the rifle held to the shoulder, at the ready, Brodie felt a familiar feeling return. It was from his time in the Army of the South as a platoon sergeant. Twenty years may have passed since then, but that mix of apprehension of the unknown, excitement of the fight ahead, and confidence that he was the better man, removed the debilitating fear that can paralyse the mind. He also felt a strong sense of responsibility and that was also familiar. Once it had been for the soldiers under his charge, now it was for just one person, Chastity. His desire to protect and keep her safe came upon him as an urgent need to remove any hostility that may threaten her, and to do that he would have to kill.

When Brodie took off his uniform for the last time in '65, it was with a desire to leave behind all that had gone before – the loss of life and the emptiness it brought to families; the battlefield injuries that took away limbs and left once strong men dependent; and the cluttered minds that drove some insane. He wanted to quarantine his past. Of course, that was easier said than done. The futility of war weighed heavy. What possible purpose had it served? Yet now, here, edging forward in the dark, the experience of fighting and killing was an indispensable advantage. Especially as it was one man against three.

Brodie kept close to the right-hand side of the ravine's vertical wall as he carefully placed each foot upon the ground to silence the slightest sound. Yet, every step didn't seem to bring him any closer to the sounds of his prey. This feeling of frustration was heightened by his failure to have walked all of this ground well before nightfall. His short reconnaissance had mostly been in the dark, and now he remained in the dark as to what lay ahead. What he had been able to confirm then was a change of direction by the ravine to the right, some one hundred paces on. Yet now, he was past that distance and still advancing, while the sounds remained at a constant distance. This led Brodie to conclude that he was actually following men on the move, traveling slowly at night to make their escape. He quickened his pace, finally changing direction with the ravine to hear the soft thud of hooves.

They were near, very near.

Brodie stopped, knelt, rifle butt to the ground as he waited for a moment while taking in deep breaths. He knew in his gut it was them. The men who had killed the Olsen family and defiled Hannah before her murder. The men who had shot Frederick Klutter in cold blood as he tried to defend and warn his daughter. The same men who had threatened to do to Chastity what they had done to Hannah.

He rose slowly to his feet and began to walk forward. He quickened his steps into a jog and after one hundred paces he broke into a run. Fifty paces on from that and gathering more speed, he went into a full sprint, rifle at the ready, legs pumping, chest heaving, dashing deep into the dark, ready to engage. Ready to kill.

Only to find nothing.

When he finally came to a halt, after covering another three hundred paces, Brodie was completely spent. Sinking to his haunches in the darkness, he sucked in gulps of cool night air into burning lungs. Somehow, those he had launched himself at, had just vanished, and he was at a complete loss as to what was going on. He remained crouched for another ten minutes, hearing not a sound. No thud of hoofs upon the ground, no muffled voices in the air. Nothing.

It was a bewildering situation, alone in the dark, with just the sound of his heavy breathing. He slowly stood, the sweat running down his temples as he marked the ground close to the ravine wall with the heel of his boot before beginning his return journey, counting each step, some 650 by the time he arrived back at their overnight camp.

Chastity was kneeling, watchful, with the pistol in her hand. Crouching down beside her, he could see and hear her apprehension as she asked, 'Did you see them?'

'No,' said Brodie.

'Where did they go?'

'I have no idea. They just seemed to disappear.'

'How can that be?'

'I just don't know, but you did hear them, didn't you?'

'I did,' confirmed Chastity.

'We'll follow their tracks at first light and do our best to catch up quickly. Hopefully, we'll be able to surprise them and attack from the rear.' Brodie waited, expecting a response, a confirmation of his intentions.

Chastity remained silent and pensive.

He prompted her. 'You OK with that?'

Chastity didn't answer immediately, leaving Brodie to wonder what was the matter, before she said, 'I think it best that we just turn around and leave?'

He was surprised and had to ask, 'Why?'

Once again Chastity was slow in her response. 'You were gone for such a long time.'

'Not that long, just half an hour or thereabouts.'

'No, it was much longer than that. Several hours.'

'No,' said Brodie, 'just a half hour, no more.'

Chastity shook her head. 'Look at the sky, it's getting light.'

Brodie looked directly up, then back at Chastity; her features now clearly visible. It made no sense. He was good at estimating time; it was why he had never bothered with a timepiece. It was around midnight when he left, at the latest it would now be one o'clock, yet the first light of a new day was breaking and that meant it was around five. How could he have possibly lost four hours?

Brodie's confusion showed on his face and Chastity lay her hand on his cheek as if to provide comfort. 'I was worried that you weren't coming back, and if you hadn't, it would have been my fault. It made me realize how selfish I had been in demanding that you try and put right that which no man can. I've been doing some thinking and killing won't bring back my father or those other poor souls. The Good Lord saved me by sending you, and for that I am more than blessed.'

Brodie was only half listening as he tried to figure out how he had managed to lose all track of time. 'Maybe you'll change your mind once the sun is up.'

'No,' said Chastity, 'I've seen my error. I now accept that I was foolish. Trying to do the Lord's work for him is an arrogance that needs chastising. I think I should be put over a knee and spanked for my infant ways.'

'I think you're a bit old for that,' said Brodie with a smile, in the hope that it would help to lighten the moment a little.

'I've been told some husbands do it regular to their wives when they step out of line. Maybe you should do it to me.'

Brodie, still confused at how hours of time could be so easily lost, was now totally perplexed with Chastity's proposal that he spank her for being juvenile. He wasn't sure what to say, other than, 'I've never laid a hand on any of my mules, so I certainly don't plan to do so to a lady.'

'Your mules have more sense than me.'

'Probably more sense than both of us,' he conceded. 'But that's still no excuse for administering the paddle to a woman.'

'You are an uncommonly gentle man, Robert Brodie.'

'I don't know about that. I just remember my manners. The ones my mother and my sisters taught me.'

'And they taught you well. Still, it doesn't necessarily need to be a paddle. The slap of a bare hand upon the more padded parts of the anatomy could well be sufficient to remind both parties of the values associated with compliance and obedience.'

Brodie's mouth opened and his tongue also moved, but not a word came forth. His brain was still trying to catch up with what he thought he had just heard.

As if from nowhere sunlight lit up the far wall of the ravine to make it glow a rich gold. A new day had begun.

On packing up, Brodie asked, cautiously, if Chastity was certain that she wanted to go back.

She did.

'Before we leave, I just want to walk the ground in daylight to where I went in the dark.'

'I'll come with you.'

'We'll all go.'

Brodie, leading Sergeant Smith, counted the steps back up the ravine to where it turned and widened, and further on to the number of 650. There, close to the wall was where he had dug his heel deep into the ground. 'I don't understand it,' he said. 'I've seen no tracks, yet we heard horses!'

'Did the sound travel from another one of the nearby ravines?' asked Chastity.

'I wouldn't have thought so, but it's the only explanation.'

Chastity looked around at the tall walls. 'Or maybe, it's just this place.'

Brodie began to turn the mules around when Corporal Jones began to sniff the wind. Brodie felt the light warm breeze upon his face just before he heard the neigh of a horse up ahead. With one slick movement he drew the Winchester from its scabbard and handed his Colt to Chastity. 'It's them,' he said.

THIRTEEN

THIS PLACE OF HELL

Indian Wind

We all want a little justice, a little fairness in the way we are treated. Trouble is, sometimes you just have to suck up the injustice and unfairness that comes your way and swallow it down like a spoonful of cod liver oil. Fortunately, most grievances in life are small and really no more than an inconvenient annoyance. For Chastity, it could occur when waiting in line at the general store, only to have someone push in and buy that last slice of apple pie. The one she'd been thinking about all day. It would make her steam. Nonetheless, being a good Christian, she would bite her tongue or say 'darn' under her breath and cool down.

Of course, some grievances can fester if not resolved and result in thoughts of revenge. Like when Chastity had cleaned Mrs Blackmores's house from top to bottom, only to be underpaid for her hard work. Boy was she sore. And then there are the thoughts of real revenge. The type where punishment is served slowly and with a fair share of pain for good measure.

When Chastity sat huddled in her little cave, she got to experience what thoughts of real revenge felt like. It didn't happen straight away. The suddenness of the pistol shot that took her father from her resulted in sheer fright and made her run like the wind. When she squeezed through that tiny entrance into that cavern, she quickly went into shock. With her knees drawn up under her chin, a chill engulfed her. One that made her shake and begin to weep uncontrollably. When she heard sounds right outside her little hideaway, she buried her face into the crook of her arm to suppress any sound while she held her breath. The call from one of Jake's men to enquire if someone could actually fit through such a small opening caused her to slightly wet herself with fear. When she finally heard them walk away, she started to whisper into her arm, 'Deliver me from evil Oh Lord, deliver me from evil, please send someone to save me. Send me a Christian traveller, a good Samaritan, one who will take good care of me.'

That night, in fitful snippets of sleep, she dreamt that a voice from on high had said, 'I will send to you a good and noble man.'

117

'Who will he be?' she had replied.

'He will be the one I send,' said the voice.

'How will I know this noble man?' she asked.

'You will know him from your sweet dreams.'

She woke with a start. The voice of Brodie coming back to her. 'May you achieve all your sweet dreams, Miss Klutter.'

'Sweet dreams,' she said quietly. 'That has to be Robert Brodie. You are sending me Robert Brodie. Oh, thank you, thank you.' And for each hour of her vigil she prayed, 'God speed Robert Brodie, my white knight.'

***

Chastity was so close to Brodie that she kept bumping into him as they slowly and quietly crept forward. Some forty paces on, a second ravine opened to their right and upon the ground the hoof prints of a horse could be clearly seen. Another twenty paces up, and just around a sharp bend, her eyes caught sight of what she thought was a pile of rags.

She looked closer, tilting her head a little. It was a man. He sat slumped against the ravine wall, the ground around him soaked red. 'He's one of them,' she said. 'Is he alive?'

They advanced until they were alongside. Brodie nudged with his boot. The wounded man opened his eyes and immediately became hysterical.

'Indians,' he said, his eyes wide with panic. 'We were trying to get through to the foothills but got lost in this warren.' His speech was fast and frantic. 'That's when they started tracking us. Been in here for over three days, but we couldn't shake them off or find our way out.'

'Indians? What Indians?' asked Brodie.

'I don't know what tribe,' he was panting as he spoke, 'but they are the wildest savages I have ever come across.'

'More savage than you?' said Chastity. 'Seems to me you just met your own kind.'

'What did these savages look like?' asked Brodie.

'Never got to see. Only attacked in the dead of night, silently, like the wind.'

Brodie looked down at the large patch of glistening blood that extended from the stomach to the knees. 'Shot? Have you been shot in the gut?'

'No, I got cut real bad, down below, where no man ever should. Had to tie a bootlace around what was left to try and stop bleeding. But no matter how tight I pulled; it wouldn't stop.'

Brodie tuned his head towards Chastity. 'Seems you started something,' he whispered.

'I know I ain't going live. No man would want to, but I don't want to die like this either, I don't deserve to, I never did wrong, I just went along for the ride. It was all Jake's doing. I don't want to go to the Lord in a state like this.'

119

'What makes you think you're going see the Lord?' shouted Chastity with fierce anger. 'And stop the trash about just going along for the ride – that's sin enough – you rode bad. You'll be on your way to that other place to see—'

Brodie patted her leg to settle her fury as he interrupted by saying, 'And you say you never got to see these Indians?'

He shook his head. 'No, only attack at night, at its blackest. Come in quiet, on foot, fast.'

'But you got some shots away, didn't you?'

'Didn't have a chance.'

'When did this happen to you?

'Just after midnight, out of nowhere, came running in, full on.' His breathing was beginning to labour as he spoke. 'Right between us. No noise, no yelling, just slashing.'

'How many were there?'

'Never sure.' His eyes glanced back and forth in fright between Brodie and Chastity. 'Seemed like many, then one, then none. They were everywhere, then nowhere. Ghosts, and all the while they were playing with our minds. Waiting. Watching. Getting ready to attack.'

'There were three of you, right?'

'No, just me and Jake.'

'Just two? But you started out as four.'

He nodded. 'They got Chad first. We should have buried him, not just left him there with his pants down, but Jake said no, we need to get out of here and save ourselves. Then they got Leland. That left just me and Jake. The two of us.'

'How did they get Leland? With a gun or a knife?'

The man was beginning to grimace as he spoke. 'A knife, same as Chad and me. Just Jake left now and he's real spooked about the Indians, on account of what he done to those Navajo girls a couple of months back near Tucson. One of them, the last one, said she had put a curse on him. He laughed it off but she said it would follow him like the wind. That he could never escape. We ribbed him about it and called it the Indian Wind till he told us to shut up. I knew then it was getting to him.'

'So why didn't you just go, get out of here and continue east?' asked Brodie.

'We tried but all we seemed to do was just go around in circles. We even tried taking our chances and going up on the surface at night.' He grimaced again. 'It was no good. Leland's horse fell down one of the ravines, rolled over on him then bolted. Left Leland unable to walk.' He now began to pant. 'Me and Jake went to find his horse, but it was long gone. Then we couldn't find our way back. We could hear Leland calling but just couldn't find him until morning, and by then they had got to him.' His speech now slowed like a tired drunk with slurred words as he said, 'This place is like hell. It haunts you and sends you in the wrong direction, it—' The man's head slumped forward as he fell into unconsciousness.

'Is he dead?' asked Chastity.

'Not yet, but it won't be long with the amount of blood he's lost.'

'Indian Wind?' asked Chastity. 'Do you believe all that being cursed stuff?'

'Don't know. Men do hallucinate when badly wounded. It seems to have convinced Jake that there is something out there after them, and him in particular.'

Chastity pulled a face, screwing up her nose. 'I say we go, now.'

'I think so too. We will still need to keep on guard for Jake, he's around here somewhere.' Brodie glanced down at his waist. 'Best I keep my knife handy too. Do you still have it?'

'No, you left me with your pistol last night,' said Chastity, twisting a little to look behind Brodie. 'You have it with you, it's on your belt.'

Brodie felt for the knife. 'Strange, I was sure that I gave it to you.' He grasped the handle and lifted it from the scabbard, exposing the polished steel. The blade was wet with blood. He quickly pushed the knife back home and spontaneously sucked in a short breath through clenched teeth.

'Something the matter, Robert?'

'We should get out of here once and for all.'

Chastity sensed something was worrying Brodie. 'Are we in danger?'

'Don't know, but something strange is going on here.'

'I feel the same,' said Chastity. 'I know we killed one, not three. And if there are a bunch of savages in here, I say best we leave them to hunt down Jake.'

'I agree,' said Brodie. 'If this is some kind of hell, it is the best place to leave him.'

'What if we do run into him?'

'We will handle it. He'll be outnumbered and I doubt if he has the stomach for a fight. Not now. Seems he's been spooked and is running scared.'

'Do we just go back the way we came?' asked Chastity.

'That's the general idea, but—'

'But what?'

'There were a lot of twists and turns on the way in. This may take a little longer than just trying to retrace our steps.'

'We couldn't have gone more than three or four miles into these gullies, altogether, could we?'

'I'm thinking it could be as much as five,' said Brodie.

'Then how big is this maze?' asked Chastity.

'I wouldn't be surprised if it is over twenty miles long and maybe as wide.'

'Best we follow our tracks back to the start,' declared Chastity.

'In some places we weren't leaving much in the way of tracks as the ground was so hard, and there were very few familiar landmarks or distinctive features. Something usually catches my eye even in the most barren of places, but I've seen nothing of note. Just keeping the sun in position has been difficult. I've never come across any place like this before in my life.'

Chastity's brow creased. 'You're starting to worry me, Robert. You speak as if we are in some kind of trap.'

FOURTEEN

THE BLOOD TRAIL
Feathers

Chastity had asked if they should wait until the unconscious man was dead so they may bury him.

After condemning the man to hell, she now proposed a burial. Curious, thought Brodie, while giving the proposition consideration, only to say abruptly, 'No.'

'Isn't that being unchristian?' she asked.

Brodie came within a hair's breadth of saying, 'Chastity, something is very wrong here. Two men have been cut up, pretty much like you cut up the first one, and we have no idea who did it, so let's just get the hell out of here and worry about being a good Christian later.' But he didn't. Instead, he just said. 'I don't think he's Christian enough to deserve a Christian burial,' which seemed to satisfy Chastity.

On turning the mules around and passing an adjoining ravine, where the hoof prints of a lone horse were upon the ground, Corporal Jones stopped and began to sniff the air.

Brodie's head dropped before he looked up and said, 'Not again, not now.'

'What is it?' asked Chastity.

Sergeant Smith now started to sniff the air, lifting his head high.

'The mules are on to something. They are smelling the air.'

'For what?'

'I have no idea.'

'Should we investigate?'

Brodie glanced down the second ravine and was feeling a little agitated. 'No, I don't think so.'

'Were those marks there before?' asked Chastity.

Brodie looked down on the ground beyond the hoof prints at drag marks that disappeared into the ravine.

'What are they from?' questioned Chastity.

Brodie couldn't understand why he hadn't seen them earlier. They were clear and he knew how they had been made. They were from the boot heels as a body was being hauled by the upper torso. He didn't want to tell Chastity, instead, he just said, 'Let's go, let's get out of here,' and pulled on the lead, only Sergeant Smith wouldn't budge. Brodie jerked harder and Sergeant Smith remained defiant. 'Come on you damn stubborn mule, get a move on.'

Chastity came to Sergeant Smith's defence. 'Maybe, you should just ask him nicely, Robert. Politeness is a virtue.'

Sergeant Smith shuffled side on so that he was positioned ready to enter the ravine as if to follow the drag marks.

Brodie wasn't in the mood for a lecture on being virtuous. 'Maybe, he should just turn his big fat rump around and get moving so we can get out of here.'

Corporal Jones sidled up to join Sergeant Smith as if in solidarity with his inquisitive stance.

'They seem to be telling us something. Do you think we should just take a peek? Maybe it's the best way for us to get out of here.'

Brodie doubted if it was a way out, but in all honesty, he didn't know. A warm, soft wind blew upon his face. Reluctantly, he said, 'I have a feeling that Jake is down there.'

'Waiting to kill us?' asked Chastity.

Brodie shook his head. 'No, I think he's wounded and has been dragged down there.'

'Who would have done that?'

'That Indian Wind,' was the mumbled response.

Chastity didn't quite hear. 'What was that?' she asked.

Brodie knew that he was being drawn in, but he had no idea why. Was it to confront Jake or to confirm that he was mortally wounded or even dead? Or was it to meet who had dragged him away?

Did it matter? Did he need to know?

He told himself that he could live with the mystery of it all. If he could just get out of this place with Chastity and the mules, he'd be a happy man. And as for all this stuff about Divine Winds or Indian Winds or the smell of roasted almonds, well, he was willing to forget about that, too. He had found something extraordinary and unexpected in Chastity Klutter and he wanted to keep it, forever. He wanted to take this precious gift and remove it from any jeopardy. The chance to have and hold something like this in his life would never come again – of that he was sure – it was one shot only. Yet, something was drawing him in, and he knew it.

He would have to go and see. The wind told him so. 'I'll take a quick look. Just a little way down, no more. OK?'

'I'm coming with you,' said Chastity.

Brodie didn't argue. It was better to have her and the mules close by. 'You stay right behind me with Corporal Jones and take my pistol.' Brodie retained the Winchester in his right hand. 'Come on, Smithy,' he said, 'let's get this over and done with.'

Sergeant Smith's ears moved upright, and his nostrils flared in response.

'I know, I can feel it too,' said Brodie as he began to lead off in a slow walk down the ravine, followed by Chastity and Corporal Jones.

The small procession, in single file, followed the fresh drag marks, which now included dark stains made by blood. The further they progressed the larger and darker the stains appeared. Brodie counted each step and by 250 paces the walls on each side started to close in, narrowing the ravine to the point where it restricted the mules as the packs were now scraping against each side. Fifty paces further on Brodie stopped. He turned to Chastity and said quietly. 'The mules won't be able to get through. We need to back up, but I'll just take a quick look ahead to make sure there is nobody there. Hopefully it's just a dead end.'

'Don't go,' whispered Chastity, 'I don't want you to leave me on my own.'

'I just want to make sure there is no one up ahead who can jump us when we are backing up the mules,' said Brodie. 'It will just take a minute or two. If anyone comes, shout or fire a shot in the air and I'll come running.'

Chastity's eyes showed her concern. 'You won't be long, will you?'

'I have no intention of being long. Just a few minutes, no more. Once done, we'll go, get out of this place for good.' Brodie didn't wait for a response from Chastity, he turned and with his rifle at the ready, advanced down the ravine that was becoming narrower and darker. Some fifty paces down, it was not much wider than shoulder width. Yet the drag marks upon the ground remained clear. Twenty-five paces further on and, glancing back quickly, he was unable to see the mules or Chastity, and when he got to a point where he had to turn side on to continue, he was just about ready to turn around when he saw a bright light ahead.

With a little persistence, squeezing sideways down the narrow rift, the light ahead became brighter, enticing him on until, suddenly, the small gap opened into a large chamber. Sunlight streamed in from above and before him, in the centre, was a large dark patch some ten or more paces across. He took small, soft steps, looking around as he made his way forward to finally kneel at the edge of the stain and press his finger down upon the earth. It sunk in and was moist red to halfway up his finger. The amount of blood required to make such a mark was difficult to comprehend, and where was the body that it had come from? There was nothing else here. Beyond the mark, some forty paces, was a sheer wall with a very narrow vertical crack. Far too narrow for anyone to pass.

Brodie stood and looked up to the sky as if to search for the source of this puzzle. It was unfathomable. It was as if a bird, a very large bird, had flown down from the heavens and snatched up a bleeding carcass. Brodie had heard of golden eagles plucking young mountain goats from rocky spurs, but such a happening out here didn't make sense. The odd large bird that Brodie had seen over the years had remained on high as if passing over the desert on its way to where the tall trees grew in the Sierra Nevada. And the blood patch was way too large to have come from a young mountain goat. He felt a shiver run down his spine. It was time to go, to get out of this place.

As he turned, a warm wind blew in his face.

He dropped his head. 'What now?' he said, then mumbled, 'I've had enough.' Lifting his head, he called out, 'I'm not a mind reader. If this is you Tanka or White Horse or whoever, what is it you want of me?' The wind continued to blow, warm and soft. 'I'm doing my best. I have found someone who is important to me and who I want to protect, but somehow, you keep drawing me back towards Death Valley. Why?'

The wind strengthened a little and flicked the collar of his shirt.

'What is so important that you want me there? Or are you trying to tell me something? If you are, maybe I'm too dumb to understand. Or are you just fooling with me? Testing me? Punishing me? Whatever it is, can we just get it over and done with, once and for all, because I don't know if I can take much more of this. I don't know if this is real or just made up in my head.' Brodie kicked at the ground. 'If I am to be guided by the Divine Wind, then guide me.'

The flap on his shirt pocket now began to flutter as the wind got stronger. Brodie looked back to give the bloodstain one last glance before returning to Chastity and the mules, when he noticed something small in the centre of the dark earth. He couldn't recall it being there before. He stepped a little closer until his toes were touching the edge of the stain and he knew immediately what it was. He snatched the hat from his head and looked at the band. The tuft of feathers, the one placed there by Chastity, was gone.

It couldn't be, he thought. How could it be?

Cautiously, he placed his foot softly upon the blood mark and took the five steps to the centre, until he was able to reach down and pick up the little posy. He looked at it closely. It looked like his, as best as he could tell, but maybe all these adornments were identical. He placed it in his hat band, and as he did the strong scent of lavender filled this natural basilica.

Brodie lifted his hat and, giving a salute towards the heavens, put it on. As he did, a trickle of water began to slowly flow from the narrow crack in the far wall. He'd never seen anything even remotely similar before and it was mesmerizing. He was now watching a phenomenon. The water was clear and was beginning to increase in volume and run across the ground to make a stream.

For a moment Brodie thought it might be a natural spring, one that had somehow been diverted from its underground flow to now arrive here at this particular moment. He watched, spellbound, as the current increased and started to gush. He kept looking, until, in a rush, it dawned upon him. 'Hell's bells,' he shouted, turned on his heels and took off like a startled desert cuckoo back towards Chastity and the mules.

In his haste, he almost tripped and stumbled, arms flailing to the point where he nearly lost control of his

Winchester. He pushed and squeezed back through the narrow crevasse, then jumped and hopped until the ravine became wide enough for him to sprint at full speed. The distance back seemed far longer than the paces he had counted, which caused him to wonder if the mules had been backed up in preparation to leave. When he did finally sight Chastity, she was exactly where he had left her.

She looked up, a little startled and, thinking that he was being chased, lifted the revolver.

'Don't shoot, it's me, Brodie,' he gasped. 'We have to get out of here quick.'

'Is it the Indians?'

'No, but it could be worse. There must be a storm in the mountains close by, and the water is coming our way.'

'Is that bad?'

'If it's a flash flood it could be lethal. We need to back up the mules and get out of here quick. Real quick.'

FIFTEEN

THE FLOOD

Hang On

Chastity couldn't see the urgency over a storm in the mountains. It was a clear sunny day directly above her head, and besides, what if some water was coming their way? Did it matter in this dry and desolate place? It had to be way better than being chased by a bunch of savage Indians. However, if Brodie knew better, she concluded, it was best to comply and began to push Corporal Jones backwards with her free hand upon the base of his neck.

'No, give me the pistol. You take the lead on Smithy and leave Jonesy to me. Just follow,' said Brodie, who now seemed somewhat frantic and more than a little abrupt in his manner.

'Follow, how?' asked Chastity.

'Talk to him, in a calm way. Tell him to back up.'

Chastity was clearly baffled. Brodie was plainly not calm, and she was finding it somewhat alarming.

'Do what I do,' said Brodie. 'OK Jonesy, we need to back up here, good boy, there we go, nice and steady.'

Corporal Jones began to step back in the narrow gully.

Brodie looked over his shoulder. 'Now you.'

'Shoo, shoo-shoo back,' said Chastity.

Sergeant Smith remained firm.

'He won't budge.'

'Did you let him know you were talking to him by name?' Brodie looked down and he saw a thin stream of water between his boots. 'Smithy, Chastity is talking to you, now back up. We have to get out of here, quick smart.'

Sergeant Smith didn't move.

'Maybe, I should say, please?' queried Chastity.

'Smithy, get that fat rump of yours moving, now.'

Chastity stepped forward and looked straight into the large dark brown eyes. 'Smithy, would you do it for me, please?'

The long ears that had flattened to each side of the head now shot upright and Sergeant Smith began to back up.

'Thank you,' she said with sincerity.

The mules continued at a slow walking pace and as soon as the ravine was wide enough, Brodie pulled them around quickly and began to lead off with Corporal Jones at a fast stride.

On returning to the main ravine, Chastity asked, 'Which way?'

'The way we came,' said Brodie with confidence and turned up the wider gully. However, they had not travelled more than fifty steps when he stopped. He could see a narrow line of running water heading towards them. 'Have to turn back.'

'Why?'

'Water, also coming this way.'

Chastity examined the flow. 'It doesn't look like much.'

'Believe me, it will soon.'

'So which way now?'

'We only have one choice. The same way as the water, and hopefully it will lead us out of here. We have to keep ahead of the tide before it floods.'

Tide! What tide, thought Chastity. What flood? The water was not much more than a trickle, not a tide. That was until Chastity passed an adjoining ravine. It was delivering a new source of water into the main ravine – and so was the next one and the one after that. Each ravine they passed was discharging more and more water, and it was getting faster and deeper. 'Where is it all coming from?' she asked. 'It's not raining here.'

'It doesn't have to. It's coming from up in the mountains.'

'Will it keep getting stronger?' asked Chastity.

This was no time for a discussion on the probability of the one in one-thousand-year flood, but

Brodie wanted Chastity to appreciate the urgency of the situation without alarming her. 'I'd expect so,' he said, while trying not to dwell on the possible dangers that they were facing. He'd heard old-timers tell of flash floods that came out of nowhere and could inundate a mine in minutes, even before it could be evacuated. And of cabins washed away from the banks of a creek at night, with the occupants still tucked up inside. 'Need to go faster,' called Brodie as the water gushed around the heels of his boots.

This sudden rise in the water from a trickle to a stream now had Chastity's attention. 'My, my, we *are* going to get wet.'

Brodie continued to encourage. 'Faster, faster.'

'Trying,' she said, 'just, having trouble with my—'

Brodie looked back to urge Chastity on. She was holding a fistful of skirt, clenched tight, in an effort to lift the hem as she tried to run.

'Darn. Stop, wait,' she called.

'Can't, got to keep moving.'

The water had soaked the bottom twelve inches of her dress, turning it dark blue.

'Stop,' she said forcefully.

Brodie stopped and turned back to see Chastity drop the lead on Sergeant Smith, undo the back of her apron and with two hands hitch up her dress to above the knees. She then re-tied the apron strings to hold the hiked-up skirt in place. 'There,' she said, 'now we can go.'

Brodie remained at a standstill. Frozen to the spot, looking at Chastity's bare legs between the hem of her dress and the top of her ankle boots.

The water continued to swirl with menace, yet regardless of the impending danger and the urgency of the moment, his eyes remained fixed as they appreciated the beautiful curve of his loved one's legs.

'We can go now, Robert, giddy up.'

'Ah, yes,' he stumbled. 'Right, of course, giddy up.' Brodie turned back and began to walk.

'You can speed up,' called Chastity. 'I can jog along now.'

Brodie broke into a shuffle step, his mind still somewhat preoccupied with the sight of Chastity's handsome calves, while small waves from the water were being washed along in front of him as if to say, you need to get a move on.

The quickening flow of water was not coming from any incline to the ground but from the numerous new sources that streamed into the main gully. This worried Brodie. It made him feel as if they were trapped in a large drain that was now filling rapidly from all sides. He could clearly see the water level rising. It was inching up the walls and above the top of his boots.

He glanced back at Chastity, her bonnet pulled back but still tied around her neck, her head lowered to look at the water splashing around her legs as she jogged. A small pebble slipped into his boot to lodge at the back of his heel. It was as annoying as hell, but he couldn't stop, there wasn't time. They had to get out and fast.

The sound of the water was also increasing, and after another ten minutes, the torrent had reached up to the back of their legs, helping to propel each of them forward. When the gully widened, Brodie hoped that the current of the muddy water would slow. But it didn't. Instead, it just seemed to accentuate the volume by forming a central ridge in the wash of the torrent, peaking and dipping as if in a show of strength. Vast amounts of water were now draining into their ravine, returning the ancient gorge into a wild river.

When the water level rose to well above the knees, Brodie began to lose his footing and was just about to call to Chastity to hang on to Sergeant Smith's breast collar when she was swept into the back of his legs, knocking him over. The rushing water now made it difficult for him to find his feet, so he hung on to Jonesy's lead and grabbed for Chastity, seizing a handful of hair to lift her head above the turbulence. 'Grab, my wrist,' he shouted.

She did.

He let go of her hair and twisted his hand to fasten to her wrist, drawing her in towards him, while calling for her to grab the harness of Corporal Jones.

Chastity flung her free arm out, taking three attempts before she was able to latch on a strap.

'Don't let go.' Brodie had to yell above the noise of the rushing water as he looked back to see Smithy

139

being propelled along, the water now cresting over his rump. He thrust an outstretched arm into the water in the hope that he could find the lead strap. 'Come on Smithy, keep coming to me.' Sergeant Smith's ears had flattened, while the whites of his eyes showed his distress. Me too, thought Brodie, not the place I want to be. His hand reached again for the strap and he felt it, briefly, clutched, but missed. He kept snatching his hand in the water, searching.

The swirling torrent had turned dark brown and was gritty to the skin. This was now a river in full flood and Brodie's feet could no longer touch the bottom. The immediate concern was that the packs would drag the mules down, to drown under the weight of the supplies. 'Come on, Tanka, give me that damn lead.'

He felt it, then it was gone. He felt it again, then gone again. Once more and he made a grab. 'Got it, Smithy,' he called as he pulled himself forward against the current, and as if to assist, Sergeant Smith lifted his head. It was just enough for Brodie to lunge and latch onto the chest harness, where he could pull himself to the side of the mule. Straight away he began to tug on the rope ties to release parts of the load and bulk of the pack. Some items, like the biscuit tin and his bedroll, quickly fell away, to be swept past him, but the soaked canvas cover made it impossible to do any more. Brodie held on tight as he called again to Tanka for his assistance. He urgently needed to get to Chastity, whose head he could see bobbing low in the water some twenty yards ahead. He feared that she was close to going under.

If only she could hang on.

It was as if the dam had burst. They were in the midst of a flooding river and the volume of water was furiously fast and spread over a width of more than one hundred yards, and it was carrying them wide apart. Between gulps of air and moments of being fully submerged, Brodie was only able to catch glimpses of Chastity as she was swept further away while he desperately clung to Sergeant Smith. The sickening realisation was now coming to him, if Jonesy went under, then so too would Chastity. He fought to pull himself higher on the harness so that he could see. The effort was almost beyond him and by the time his head was well clear of the water, they had gone.

Rolling on to his back to gulp in some breaths between mouthfuls of water, Brodie noticed that to each side the banks were now low, leaving him to hope that they had actually been spat out of the maze. If not, there seemed little hope. They were now like flotsam with the possibility of being washed to the bottom. Or had that already happened to Chastity and Corporal Jones?

Brodie's boot struck ground.

He was sure of it as he kicked down to confirm that it had actually happened. He and his mule were now slowing and turning in a swirling eddy as the roar of the river started to diminish. Smithy lifted for a second or two; he had also found the bottom. Brodie kicked and felt his foot hit the river bed. At the top of his voice he yelled out to Chastity, 'Hang on, it's getting shallow, hang on.' His eyes desperately searched the surface of the water but he couldn't see her, and he guessed she couldn't hear him either.

SIXTEEN

THE SKIDOO

Till Death Do Us Part

By the time Sergeant Smith was able to find a firm footing and hold fast against the draining water, Brodie was near to exhaustion. He retained his grip on the harness and eventually, as the water receded, he swivelled around to sink down and sit upon a wide mudflat. The water was still flowing across his lap as he now faced back towards the source of the flood. It was difficult for him to get a feel for just how far they had been swept downstream, but from this vantage point it looked to be many, many miles. He was unable to make out any of the ravines and looking to the left and the right, it was as if he had been dumped in the middle of a river delta where the tide had just gone out with a rush. The water around him now pooled

143

and was draining away quite quickly. Slowly, he pulled himself to his feet and as he looked around he was surprised at just how close he was to the mountain foothills. However, no matter how hard he searched the landscape, nowhere could he see Chastity.

He pulled up the waterlogged canvas cover that was draped over to one side and patted a hand on Sergeant Smith's neck before taking the lead. Some five hundred paces down, and towards a large rocky outcrop, he could see where the water flowed around to the left. With each step, he became fearful as to what lay ahead. He braced himself, glancing down at his boots to whisper, if there be a Divine Wind, please let me find Chastity alive. A warm, soft breeze touched his face and it lifted his spirits.

The aroma of lavender came just before he caught sight of Chastity and Corporal Jones further down, about three hundred yards away on the far bank. She was waving frantically to get his attention. He waved back with enthusiasm and directed his mule, saying, 'Over to Jonesy and Chastity and then we can rest up.'

The final barrier was a narrow channel where the water was still draining quickly. As he stepped into the stream, it went up to his neck and it gave him a brief fright. Sergeant Smith worked hard to complete the crossing, using his power to pull them both up onto the bank, which came with a sense of relief for Brodie. He waved again to Chastity, who was now some two hundred paces ahead.

At fifty paces he called, 'You OK?'

Chastity was still holding on to the lead as if tethered to Corporal Jones, and as he drew closer, she said back to him, 'Soggy. You?'

'Happy,' he said with a grin. 'Happy just to see you in one piece, even if you are bit soggy.'

'A bit?' said Chastity and as they drew near, she slipped under his outstretched arm. 'Give me a hug,' she said.

This surprised Brodie but he responded and enclosed his arm around her shoulder. 'Cold?' he asked.

'No, not really, just need a hug, that's all.'

'OK,' he said with a little hesitation.

She pressed in tight against him.

Brodie's began to pat her upper arm with his hand.

Chastity looked up. 'It's a loving hug I want from you Robert, not paternal comfort from an old uncle. Put some effort into it.'

He tightened his arm around her and squeezed, immediately becoming aware that he could feel her bosom against his chest.

'That's a bit better,' she said and wriggled in a little closer.

Brodie self-consciously looked down and could clearly see the outline of Chastity's breasts through the wet fabric. He was about to release his grip out of a sense of modesty; however, it was clear that Chastity felt no such inhibitions. She lay the side of her face against his chest and nestled in, and awkwardly he continued to hold her tight.

'I used to like swimming and thought I was pretty good at it,' said Chastity quietly, 'but if it hadn't been for Jonesy, I'd would have been a goner.'

'When did you go swimming?' asked Brodie, trying to make small talk.

'When I was little. All the kids did. Haven't done it for years. Used to be such fun skinny dipping.' Chastity looked up at Brodie. 'I loved that fairy tale book about the water babies too. I wanted to be one. But I've got to tell you Robert, I didn't feel like any water baby out there. I just felt like a drowned rat.'

Brodie wanted to say something to match Chastity's easy manner. He felt comfortable and free around this gal and she was definitely comfortable around him. The difference was, she could express it, while he just couldn't find the words.

As they stood in their embrace the sun shone down upon them from a clear sky, and the torrents of water dwindled away. It was as if the menace of the flood had just been some dreamlike illusion. Brodie shifted his weight from one wet boot to the other, while Chastity remained perfectly still, except for a tiny nuzzle of her face to scratch an itching nose by rubbing it against his shirt.

In an effort to sound relaxed and in charge, Brodie said, 'It wasn't that bad.'

Chastity lifted her head and said, 'What do you mean it wasn't that bad? I thought I was going to

146

drown, and I didn't want that to happen. I wanted to live. I thought that maybe you might drown, and I didn't want that to happen either.'

Brodie, partly out of misguided need to show manliness, while not understanding the importance of silence when a woman is declaring her fears and affection, began to interrupt with the protest of, 'Oh, no that would never—'

She cut him short. 'And if that had happened, I would have willingly gone under.'

Brodie, a little confused as to what Chastity was saying, didn't know if he should continue to protest or seek clarification. Thankfully, he did neither. He'd heard what she had said, that she didn't want to live if he didn't live.

The air seemed to exhaust from his lungs and his chest sunk. As difficult as it was for him to put his feelings into words, standing there, right at that moment and holding Chastity Klutter, he felt the same. Had she gone under the wash; he too would have wished to join her. It was as if she was now part of him and he slowly pulled her closer, while lowering his chin until his lips touched upon her damp fair hair. Quietly, he said, 'Till death do us part.'

***

They tramped down the side of the river bed with Chastity making it clear that she wanted her hand held. Along the way they found some of their

147

missing items, like Brodie's bed roll and the biscuit tin. 'Lucky,' she said, tucking it under her arm.

'It's empty,' said Brodie.

'Of biscuits, but I put my Bible in there to keep it safe. Don't know what I'd do if I'd lost the Holy Scriptures.'

Brodie decided not to announce that it was one of the items that had come free when he was trying to jettison the pack from Sergeant Smith's back. So, he just said, 'Smart thinking. Nice and safe.'

'Do you know where we are, by chance?' asked Chastity.

'I do,' said Brodie, 'right to the front of us is the Panamint Range and just over there, between those two peaks, is the Skidoo Pass.'

'The Skidoo, really?' said Chastity. 'That's where my father and I were heading. That was our dream. I didn't know we were so close.'

'Nor did I,' said Brodie. 'All I knew was that we were on the Mojave side of the range but not this near.' He pointed a little to the right. 'Over that mountain ridge there, about twenty miles, is Furnace Creek.'

'Is that where we're going?'

'It would make good sense. We can resupply there. May even be able to hitch a ride back to Mojave on one of the borax wagons.'

'You know lots of people there, don't you?'

'Know them all.'

'Will they be surprised to see you?'

Brodie couldn't help but smile. 'You bet they will.' Especially with you by my side, he thought.

'So, they weren't expecting to see you back?'

'Nope.'

'Will you stay?' The question from Chastity came with a degree of uncertainty.

'No,' said Brodie. 'As soon as we can get fixed up, we should go.'

'For the best,' said Chastity and squeezed Brodie's hand. 'The pass, is it difficult to cross?'

'Not on foot. Bringing a wagon train down the other side now, even when empty, is tricky.'

'Why?'

'The track is cut up bad. The last time I came over, I nearly fell off.'

'The pass or the wagon?'

'Both.'

'Lucky,' said Chastity.

'You don't know half of it,' he mumbled.

Chastity's eyes were fixed on the mountains when she asked, 'So where would the mine be that my father inherited from my uncle? Close by?'

'Be around here somewhere. I would have to see the claim to say where exactly.'

'I can show you.' Chastity stopped and started to ease the lid from the biscuit bin. 'It's with the Bible, but I can't get this darn lid off.'

Brodie offered to help. 'Let me hold the base. You put your hands around the lid.' He held it in position for her. 'No, don't pull. Twist, while I twist in the other direction.' Slowly the lid came free along with a little water.

'How could any water get in there?' asked Chastity, 'when the lid was on so tight.' She pulled out the Bible that was damp and turned to the back where the registered claim was neatly folded. It was damp and as she opened it up, she exclaimed, 'Darn, darn, darn.' The handwritten blue ink upon the printed form had run.

'Just open it carefully and lay it on the lid to dry. It won't take too long, and we are in no hurry.'

When Chastity could safely hold it up to the light, it was almost impossible to read where the form had been filled out.

Brodie lent in; their heads so close as to touch. 'It was issued in Mojave so the registration number will allow you to replace it,' he said optimistically.

'I don't think that will be necessary. My father always had his doubts if it was going to yield anything of note. It was really my dream so that we could purchase an orange orchard in Crafton. Would have been nice to visit the mine, though, just for a look.'

'I can't make out the location,' said Brodie, 'and I've never heard of anyone named Klutter working a claim anywhere in Death Valley, let alone the Skidoo.'

'Oh, my uncle's name was not Klutter. He was my mother's brother. His surname was Derwent.'

'Larry Derwent?' asked Brodie.

'Well, we all called him Uncle Lawrence, not Larry, on account of him being so esteemed.'

'Esteemed or stern? I would have called him—' Brodie stopped mid-sentence. He was starting to learn when best to keep his thoughts to himself around Chastity.

'Go on,' she said.

'Let's just say he was not known for his sunny disposition. Even when he did make a little profit.'

'Little?' questioned Chastity. 'He made a good profit. Built a big house. Well, big by my estimations.'

'Did he ever marry?' asked Brodie.

'No,' said Chasity. 'He was never really popular with the ladies, even the gold diggers had trouble warming to him.'

Brodie decided it was best not to add to the good judgement of others, regardless of their intentions.

'But you knew him?' asked Chastity.

'I knew of him, kind of. He kept to himself. Never drank or played cards. The money he made from his mine was early on, or at least we all thought that was the case. He worked his claim till his health gave way and left. Gee, that would have to be close to fifteen years ago.'

'That would be right,' said Chasity still trying to read the claim without success. 'Fancy you knowing him.'

'Yep,' said Brodie as he rubbed two fingers over the stubble on his chin. 'Know something else, too.'

'What's that?' asked Chastity, still reading.

'Know where his mine is. Do you want to see it?'

Chastity's head flicked up to look at Brodie. 'Do I?' she said with excitement. 'Do I ever.'

SEVENTEEN

THE OLD MINE

Swing a Pick

The route to the old mine had changed little over the years. There was some extra growth from the creosote, but that was about all. Brodie even caught sight of the lone Joshua tree, which was exactly as he remembered it with its straight sturdy trunk and upstretched arms with fists of light and dark green needle points. 'Not far,' he called over his shoulder.

Chastity was looking at the view. 'It's kind of pretty up here but where is everyone? Where are the neighbours?'

'You don't get neighbours out here, Chastity. This is difficult country and all the water has to be carried in, every last drop of it. Very few are willing to make this place home, even for one season.'

'My father said we could rely on our neighbours to help us out once we got here.'

'Who told him that?'

'My uncle, I think.'

Brodie had to stop himself from saying, maybe Larry Derwent did have a sense of humour after all – even if only to pull a leg.'

Half a mile on, Brodie declared, 'This is it.'

Chastity looked about as her enquiring expression quickly changed to one of being mightily unimpressed on sighting the mine entrance. 'Doesn't look like much. Very small, you need to duck your head just to get through the door.'

'Most mining is done on your knees, unless you go deep and bring in the mules. Your uncle never used mules. Regardless, I do know that he did pull some nuggets out of here not that long after he started digging. Trouble was, the deeper he went, the less he found. Or at least that's what everybody believed.'

'Would have been difficult getting all those nuggets out of here without mules. What did he use, a wheelbarrow?'

'Wheelbarrow! No, he'd just put them in his pocket or the end of a sock.'

'Pocket? Sock?' exclaimed Chastity. 'I thought nuggets were big and they had to be lifted with two hands.'

Brodie clicked his tongue before asking, 'Did Larry tell your dad that, too?'

'I guess that's where it came from.'

'All the nuggets I've ever seen in my life are small. Still valuable though.'

'How small?' asked Chastity.

'Fit comfortably onto the face of a coin.'

'Big coin or little coin?'

'An Indian head cent.'

'No, that can't be. A one cent coin, that's bitty. I've seen photographs of gold nuggets. I've seen Oliver Martin with his nugget. The one sent to him by God.'

Brodie pressed his lips tight before answering. He knew the story of Martin, everyone did, and his 103-pound nugget, and how he had credited his good fortune to God. But Chastity's expectations were more than a little unrealistic and a little worrying. If she had planned to fly to the moon by flapping her arms, it would have held more credence. However, he wanted to let her down gently. 'A gold nugget, regardless of the size, is still a gold nugget. One that weighs just one ounce is worth twenty dollars. Get five and you have one hundred dollars. Not bad.'

'So, you just have to dig up lots of little ones?'

'Well,' said Brodie, 'that's kind of the gist of it, yep.'

'Have you ever dug up five nuggets?'

'Sure have,' said Brodie with more than a little pride.

'How long did it take?'

'A month.' In truth, it had taken the best part of two, but what's two months out of two hundred spent prospecting?

'That's way too long. I'd prefer just one big one, quickly.'

'Wouldn't we all,' lamented Brodie. 'Do you want to take a look inside?'

Chastity poked her head into the opening. 'Dark. Are there snakes in there?'

'Could be.'

Chastity kept looking into the gloom. 'Then I'm not going in.'

Brodie could feel her disappointment. 'Seen enough?' he asked.

'Guess.' It came out in a crestfallen tone.

Brodie realised that the bubble of her dreams had now been well and truly punctured. By bringing her here, hopefully, it would now make the decision to return to San Bernardino much easier.

'Can I just dig one little hole?' she asked. 'I'd like to do it for my father. Especially, if he's looking down on us.'

'Of course, I'll get the pick for you.'

'Won't I just need the shovel?'

'The ground is way too hard. Just take a swing of the pick, then shovel away the spoil, and we'll go.'

Chastity gave a nod in agreement.

Brodie got the pick and handed it to Chastity. As she took it in her hand, she couldn't help but comment on the weight.

'The weight is required to crack the earth, particularly in these parts where it is hard and rocky. Now, you need to squeeze the handle when the pick strikes the ground. It will give more force and help protect your hands and the muscles in the forearm.'

'Where should I dig?'

'It's your claim. Wherever you like.'

Chastity moved across towards some rocks. Brodie thought that she was being a little too adventurous and suggested that she try a clump of earth just beside it that looked as if it had been fashioned into a small seat. Miners often made little terraces near the entrance where they could place tools or sit and rest.

'Here?' asked Chastity. 'The one that looks like a little table.'

Brodie nodded. 'I think it was a seat actually, but no one will be using it again. Unless you are thinking of taking up mining.'

'No,' said Chastity emphatically, 'I'm only going to do it just this one time.' She grasped the handle and with all her strength propelled the implement into the air.

The pick swivelled as it went to full height above her head, causing a loss of control. Sergeant Smith and Corporal Jones, feeling in danger, stomped back out of the way with haste, raising their heads to avoid decapitation. The pick, now on the way down, whizzed so close by Brodie's ear that he was able to feel the rush of air.

Chastity instantly knew that she had done wrong and dropped the tool. It spun head over handle as it cartwheeled upon the rocky ground.

The empty silence that followed was finally filled by Chastity saying, 'I don't need to do this, do I?'

The easy answer for Brodie was to say no, let's just leave it be. But a warm breeze murmured across his face and the scent of lavender wafted over him. It was a powerful reminder of how he had found Chastity in her little hideaway. She was a tough and resourceful gal, yet she was showing her tender side by wanting to do this in memory of her father. 'Let me help,' he said as he went to recover the pick. Returning to step around behind her as he whispered. 'Let's do this together, for Frederick.'

'Are you sure? I'm dangerous.'

'I know, you scared the animals.'

'If I had hit Smithy or Jonesy, I would never have forgiven myself.'

'I was referring to me also, but never mind.' He was now pressed up close behind Chastity with his arms stretched around her and the pick in his right hand. 'Now place both hands just above mine.

She did.

Brodie put his left hand above hers.

'Now, lift and put the point of the pick on the middle of the surface we are going to strike.' He guided her hands. 'OK, that's the point we are going to aim for, just like you aimed for those ducks in flight with your father's shotgun. Got it?'

Chastity gave a determined nod.

'Now we lift up, keeping the pick straight and high above the head, while never moving our sight from that little spot. Then we swing and grip tight as the pick makes contact. Ready?'

Chasity wriggled her bottom into Brodie in readiness. 'Ready,' she said.

'OK, lift.'

Chastity lifted the pick with the assistance of Brodie until it was held aloft, and at that precise moment Brodie felt a wonderful soothing warmth wrap around him. Was it from the Divine Wind?

'Go.'

The pick swung down with the force of a blacksmith's hammer upon an anvil and the point struck exactly where Brodie had told Chastity to aim.

The little pedestal of earth split open, with both halves falling to each side as if sliced in two. A large, round, solid lump, the size and shape of a cannonball, fell to the ground with a thump and raced towards their feet, causing them to jump out of the way. It came to rest some twenty feet away, leaving a groove in the ground as proof of its weight.

They walked over to the sphere until it was just inches away from their toes. Brodie looked down to where the point of the pick had gouged out a deep scar on the surface, some six to eight inches long.

'Good God,' he said in disbelief.

'Have I done something wrong again?' said Chastity in annoyance with herself.

'Good God,' repeated Brodie, his eyes wide and his mouth open.

'I have done something wrong,' said Chastity, 'I knew it. I should never have embarked on this silliness. That ball could have squashed our toes, or worse, knocked us off our feet and off this mountain.'

'I'm not sure that I would have cared,' said a mesmerized Brodie.

'Why?' asked Chastity. 'Why wouldn't you have cared?'

'Just look. That's gold.'

'Oh,' said Chastity. 'Really, are you sure?'

'I'm sure,' said Brodie, 'I've chased it for nearly twenty years, I know what it looks like and what it smells like.'

'Smell?' questioned Chastity. 'What does gold smell like?'

'Success,' said Brodie in a whisper, his eyes fixed upon the giant nugget. 'I've seen this in my dreams a thousand times or more, only it was never this big, this grand, and just look at that gleaming colour. It has to be pure, one hundred per cent solid gold.'

'Then that's good. We are rich, aren't we?'

'Rich?' said Brodie with a shake of his head in sheer astonishment. 'We have been rewarded with riches beyond belief. Beyond our dreams.'

THE END